TRIPLE BOND

Muffin Top Bakery
Book 2

TASHA HART

Regina never thought she needed a man to be happy... then Michael came. Except, he didn't make her smile with joy. No, he made her *furious*.

Sure, Regina has always been a bit stubborn and independent. That's what makes her such a good lawyer. But now she's in a bind because she has to resolve her mother's estate and, for the first time, she needs some help. She caves, puts her ego aside, and reluctantly asks for assistance…

And gets *Michael Pickett*.

Seriously? Did it have to be *him?* Sure, he's a brilliant attorney with a body to die for. And yeah, he definitely fills out a suit in the most delicious ways, but… he's the most stubborn and independent person she's ever met since…

She's looked in the mirror!

That's right. He's a male version of Regina—the two of them constantly at odds until they realize one simple thing:

Sure, they hate each other with a fiery burning passion.

But…

They might also love each other with that same intensity.

Chapter One

REGINA

It's been a couple months since Mama's funeral, and I can't say it's gotten any easier with time. Things still haven't died down yet, which has begun to really take its toll on me. I spend every single day in Mama's office trying to sort through her finances.

Everything is such a mess; it took weeks just to even get everything organized enough, so I could really look at it. Trying to get her estate settled has proven to be the most challenging. I love Mama, but I really wish she hadn't left us such a mess. It angers me sometimes that she never called me before she got sick to come out here and help out.

I fought with Bridgid all the time in the beginning about how alone and overwhelmed I was feeling, but she's so consumed in her new marriage with Joel that I don't think she really even heard me. I don't blame her. Mama's death was the hardest on her, so I try not to bother her with much anymore.

I think losing Mama really showed all of us what is really important in life. I was never really close with any of my sisters, which was mostly my fault. But lately, Trulia and I have been spending so much time together bonding and really learning about each other for once. It feels good to finally be close with her, I just hate that Mama isn't here to see it.

If things weren't good between Trulia and I right now- I don't know what I'd do. She's been helping me deal with the fact that I got let go from my job right before Mama got sick. If it were any other job it wouldn't be hitting me this hard, but I had been working there for as long as I can remember. I dedicated so many years of my life to that place, not even allowing myself to have a social life because of it. I've never been in a situation like this and it's left me in a tailspin for sure. I'm still trying to get back on my feet.

Regardless of everything, I'm just really happy that I'm finally here with my sisters after so many years of being separated. I left Texas not long after I turned eighteen, and so did Trulia. Bridgid is the only one that stayed. Of course, Tru and I still visited for the holidays and such- but it just wasn't the same. It's been almost twenty years since the three of us were all living in the same place. We've got a lot of catching up to do- that's for sure.

It gives Tru and I something to bond over, the fact that we both moved away from home so soon. I think I always judged her for moving to New York City to be an artist. I always just assumed she was slacking off and not really making anything of herself. Turns out she's actually amazing at what she does, and she deserves a lot more credit than she gets.

It's funny because the two of us are so opposite. I've always been more high-strung, more controlling and demanding- I can admit that. Meanwhile, Trulia has always been the easy-going, calm, go-with-the-flow type. I think that's good though- we balance each other out.

I'm in Mama's office sorting through some papers when Tru calls to me that dinner is ready. Sighing, I shove everything aside and make my way to the dining room. This has become our routine. I spend the day going through all the files and such, while she sorts through Mama's belongings and packs things up. Then she gets sad looking at all of Mama's things and starts dinner. It's really very depressing.

Tonight's menu consists of tomato soup and cheesy garlic bread- which we have at least twice a week. We sit down across from each other and dig in.

"Do you know how to make anything else?" I complain.

"Hey, you're welcome to do the cooking for once if you so please," she rolls her eyes.

"Yeah I'm not Bridgid."

"Exactly," she smirks.

We sit in silence for a couple minutes, dipping our bread into the soup.

"So how's the estate coming?" Trulia breaks the silence.

"Honestly? I'm so fucking overwhelmed. I have no clue how things got so messed up. I really don't think I can sort everything out on my own. It's a disaster, Tru."

"I'm sorry… I wish I could help."

"Trust me, you are helping," I shoot her a smile. "Just being here with me is helping… I don't know what I'd do if you weren't here with me every day."

"Well good, I'm glad. Maybe Bridgid can offer some help?"

"I don't think we should bother her… she was the one here with Mama every day. I look at it like this is our payback for leaving. She deserves some time to just sit back and enjoy her life. Besides, I don't want to disrupt her and Joel's bubble."

"I understand. I'm sure she would appreciate you thinking of her. I try not to even mention what's going on over here during our weekly calls. I don't want to upset her."

"My how the tables have turned," I sigh.

Trulia nods, finishing up the rest of her soup.

"I have faith in you, Reggie. You're gonna get it all figured out, I know it."

I wish I believed in myself the way she does. Because right now I'm about ready to throw my hands up. I clean up the table while Tru does the dishes, and head back to Mama's office for another long night.

Chapter Two

REGINA

Once again, I'm hunched over in Mama's office, scouring all of her financial documents. A few more days have gone by, and still I'm no closer to getting the estates financials figured out than I was a week or a month ago.

I wake up every single day dreading stepping into that office. It has become my least favorite place to be. I'm starting to dread the fact that I'm not going to have any of this figured out anytime soon. I fear that I may have to call in some help. I don't want to; I want to be able to do this on my own- but despite my stubbornness- I think it may be time.

I can't take this for one more second. Grabbing my purse and my keys, I slide my shoes on, and head out the door.

Hopping in my car, I head to the nearest coffee shop. I down the first cup, and desperate to feel alive, go for a second.

'Bridgid would be furious at me for having coffee anywhere that wasn't the Muffin Top,' I think as I head to the bakery to see her.

'I could use some good ol fashioned Bridgid advice right about now. Here's to hoping she's in the mood for it,' I think as I pull up. I can already see her coming to greet me at the door.

We embrace right away, holding on longer than normal. It's been two weeks since we've seen each other. The three of us have a weekly call to stay in the loop, but Bridgid is usually too busy with Joel to actually hang out. I'm not bitter about it though, I completely understand where she's at right now.

"Wow, the bakery looks amazing- did you change something?" I ask.

"Actually yes! Joel just gave the walls a fresh coat a couple shades lighter than it was! Doesn't it look so much better? We also added a couple new pieces of art that he found at a local flea market. Mama never let me change anything- but it was in desperate need of some sprucing," Bridgid rambles on.

"I think it looks amazing, really. Mama would be proud."

"I think so too. She was always so against changing anything- she wanted it to have the same décor from when it first opened- but times are changing, and the bakery needs to catch up. I also added a couple new items onto the menu and took out some of the old ones! Wanna try one of the new donuts we added??"

"Sure, I'd love to!"

"Perfect, I'll have them bring one over while I make you a cup of coffee to go with it." Even though I just had two cups, I don't protest. When Bridgid is on a roll like this, I've learned to just sit back and let things happen.

"Okay, so it's a red velvet cake donut with cream cheese frosting filling." She waits for me to take a bite before continuing. "I begged Mama for years to put this on the menu, but she *hated* cream cheese anything, so she wouldn't allow it. It's delicious though, right?"

I nod in agreement, mouth completely full. It really is delicious- but I expected nothing less from Bridgid- everything she makes is amazing. I finish the rest of my donut and take a sip before getting to the reason I came.

"Okay, so I didn't just come by to check out the place," I admit.

"I figured as much, go on," she says before taking a sip of her own coffee.

'I wonder how many of those she's had today.'

"Well, as you know I've been knee-deep in Mama's financials. I have been trying and trying to get her estate organized- but I'm literally no closer than I was a month ago. I have no idea what to do- everything is a mess. Obviously, I really didn't want to bother you with any of this- which is why I've avoided even updating you on it. I love seeing how happy you are with Joel, and I don't want to stress you out- you've got enough to worry about what with running the bakery and all. But I'm at a complete loss, and I could really use some advice."

"Reggie, you can *always* come to me- I don't care what's going on- we're sisters, that's what I'm here for."

"I know, I know… but you know me, I've always had a hard time admitting when I need help. I pride myself in always doing everything alone. I've always been this way."

"Well that's gonna have to change now that the three of us are all in the same place. We've got your back Reg, and we're not going to let you drown in this," she reassures me.

After a long talk, we come to the conclusion that I need to call in some reinforcements. I decide to make a call to my friend in Chicago to see if she can come help me get this settled. Although I do feel a bit relieved knowing that I might be able to get this wrapped up quicker- I can't get rid of this nagging feeling in the pit of my stomach that I've had since we discovered the shape of things.

I head back to Mama's, but I don't even *look* in the direction of the office. Tru and I start working on dinner. No tomato soup tonight, Bridgid and Joel are coming to join us. We settle on a nice roast instead.

Once dinner is ready, we set the table for four and call Bridgid and Joel to the table. We dive into our roast, keeping the conversation light and funny, with no talk about Mama or the estate.

The four of us spend the rest of the night together, discussing everything from Bridgid and Joel's decision to start trying to have a baby, to redoing the lobby of the bakery. It's such a fun night that I don't want it to end. I don't want to have to snap back to reality tomorrow… I'm just not ready.

Chapter Three

REGINA

As soon as I wake up, the dread returns. That is, until I remember about my decision to call in help. I get up, shower, and eat some breakfast before plopping down on the couch to enjoy a peaceful moment before I make this phone call.

I actually have to remind myself to take moments to just breathe. When I don't, it becomes harder for me to hold it together. It becomes harder for me to not lash out at whoever's closest. I've even started doing a little bit of meditating in the mornings before I start my day. I can't say it's actually doing anything- but at least I'm trying.

Closing my eyes, I do some little stretches, pushing any thoughts about Mama and the estate out of my mind. I just let myself exist for a moment, breathing in and out. Once I feel calm, I head to the office and dial my friend, Livia, from Chicago. I pray that she can help me. I don't know what I'll do if it turns out she can't.

"Hello?"

"Livia! Hi, it's Reggie!"

"Reggie, wow- it's good to hear your voice. How have you been? How's Texas treatin' you?"

"I know, it's been too long since we talked on the phone. I'm doing as good as can be expected, considering. It feels good to be home, it really does- a lot better than I expected it would."

"How are you doing since your mom passed?"

"It's definitely been a struggle. Every day is a roller coaster. Actually, that's kind of why I called you."

"What's up? Is everything okay??"

I take a deep breath before continuing.

"Well- after Mama passed, we discovered that her finances were a complete mess. Her estate is in shambles. I've been going through things for weeks and weeks to no avail. I'm at a complete loss right now as to what I should do. So, I figured who better to call than the legend herself. Do you happen to have some time to come down here and help me sort through this mess?"

"Wow… that's rough, I'm so sorry. I've worked on many cases like that before. It's not easy, especially when it's your own family

member. I want to help you so bad; you know I do- unfortunately though, I'm actually not available right now. I'm currently on another tough case and there's no one that can even take over for me- I'm completely tied up. There's just no way I could come down there and give you my full attention like you need…"

My heart sinks. I really was counting on her to be able to help me out.

"… but you know I would never leave you hanging dry like that. I'll contact my colleague, Michael, and have him come down as soon as he can possibly get there. He's really good- he'll have the estate settled in no time; I promise you."

I breathe a sigh of relief.

"Oh, Livia, thank you so much. Oh my god- you have no idea how much this is going to help me. Thank you thank you thank you."

"Not a problem at all hun- I'm just sorry that I can't be there myself. But I know Michael will be a huge help, you'll barely have to lift a finger."

"Ugh, thank you- you're a lifesaver, Livia- seriously."

"I gotchu girl- I'll call Michael as soon as I hang up and then I'll text you with the details on when he'll be getting there."

"Sounds perfect!"

We chat for a bit longer, catching up about my loss of employment and a few other things. It's nice to talk to someone other than the same three people I've been talking to since coming back home. Once we hang up, I head into the kitchen to sit with Trulia while I wait to receive Livia's text.

Sinking down into my chair at the table, I let out a groan.

"What's wrong with you?" Trulia questions.

"Just exhausted is all. But I've finally got someone coming to help me out with this, I'm just waiting on the text to find out when they'll be here."

"Oh thank god, now you can stop moping around here 24/7."

"Ha-ha, don't speak too soon."

After a few minutes, my phone goes off. It's Livia with Michael's flight details and some more information about his stay. I can't even express how relieved I am to finally have some help coming. I've been going at this alone for way too long now, and no one should ever have to do this alone. It's just too depressing.

I eat a quick snack before heading back to the office to straighten everything up in preparation for Michael's arrival. I want this to go as smoothly as possible from here on out. I just hope this guy really does know what he's doing.

Chapter Four

MICHAEL

I swear I'm not uptight. People sometimes say I am, but I think it's just the type A in me shining through a little more than it should. I'm *not* uptight. I'm just not silly. Some people love to be fun and crack jokes and surround the water cooler early in the mornings before the billing hours officially start. Others are like me.

And by me, I mean they walk right by the rest of their coworkers and keep a straight trail to their office. Again, this isn't because I'm uptight but because I don't see the point in talking to people like that, not when it only wastes time and doesn't serve anything.

No, I, Michael Pickett, am not uptight. And anyone who says I am uptight is maybe just a little too loose. Really, it's not me. I glance at myself in the glass of the windows to my right, my dark short brown hair, my burnt umber eyes.

Gosh, do I look uptight? I swear I'm not. My hair just slicks back that way naturally. I don't even put gel in it. There's nothing I can really do about it. I run a hand over my hair and then begin walking again. Sighing, I check my watch. There are about seventeen minutes until work starts.

Perfect. I always like to be fifteen minutes early— not because I'm uptight but because I like to have time to settle myself. Maybe that's why people call me uptight? I'm not, though. I wave at Mallory, one of the paralegals.

Once I finish passing her, I realize I probably should have said something. Too late now. This is my usual morning: fast paced and always feeling right but slightly poorly planned, you know? I'm good at interacting with people when it comes to real estate law but not with much else. It's always been that way, I guess.

And then, when I see my boss, Livia Johnson, Esq.— and yes, we say it like that— walking towards my door, I can only hope that she's going to pass by me and go to Robert's office, the one right next to mine. Sadly, she stops right at mine.

Cursing, I begin walking a little faster, not wanting to keep her waiting, especially not with that grim look on her face. I try to smile, but it feels forced, so I drop it as I stop in front of her.

"Hey, Michael," Livia says. Her tone is light enough that it doesn't seem like I'm in trouble, but you can never fully know with Livia. After all, her mouth is still in that stern little line that it straightens into whenever she's upset about something.

"Good morning," I answer, exuding confidence. "What can I do for you?"

"Can we speak in my office please? It's something personal." She crosses her arms and pivots, walking towards her office before I can even answer.

"Sure." I stiffen as I begin walking behind her. What's this about that she won't tell me in front of others? I begin running every case I've done in the past week that could be getting me fired or something. I've cleared all of my cases, even settled one yesterday, so I don't think it's that. My performance review was just last month, and that was stellar, too.

"Okay," Livia says as she closes the door behind us. Instead of sitting behind her desk as she usually does, she sits on the end of it, her arms still crossed. Then she meets my eyes. "I need to ask you something."

"Oh, okay… Um, what?" he asks. By the way she winces, I wonder if I said things too harshly, but it's too late now, huh?

"A good friend of mine called me yesterday. She used to be the executive director of a financial firm, so she's having a hard time figuring out all the financials of the estate and everything— her mother owned a bakery. She needs some help."

"That's too bad," I remark, just grateful I'm not in trouble or anything.

"I normally wouldn't ask, but I can't break away from the Meade case over here. We have a lot of meetings lined up, and he's really stressed about everything, and I don't think I'd be able to convince him to wait for me here, so I'm tied down. Would you be able to go and help her for me? It's just really a lot, and she needs someone with your kind of expertise. It'd be paid, of course."

"Don't worry about a thing, Livia. Of course I can help. I have a few things here, but nothing pressing that I can't put on hold."

"I wouldn't ask unless it was really important. Sorry for the short notice."

"It's fine. I can go help your friend."

"Perfect. Thank you so much, Michael. I really appreciate it. You don't have to do this."

"Really, it's not a problem."

"Okay, so…" She stands and wraps around her desk, sitting down and turning her desktop on. "All the details are already arranged…" She trails off as her typing increases. One hard click. "Good. I've just sent everything over to you. Did I tell you it's all arranged? Paid?"

"Yes, you did."

"Great. So, at this point, all you have to do is pack. The flight leaves at noon. The bakery and everything is in Belton."

"As in Belton, Texas?"

"Yes. Sorry it's such short notice. I know you're uptight about these things."

"No, I'm not. Everything is good. Belton, Texas. I should probably leave to pack now, though." I am already turning around to exit.

"Thank you so much again, Michael."

"You can stop thanking me. I guess I'll see you whenever I get back."

"Yes, I'll have my friend pick you up. Her name is Regina Grant."

"Sounds good." I give her a half-salute before leaving her office. My briefcase is still in my hand, but now I'm heading back out already. Time to pack.

Chapter Five

REGINA

I pull into the parking lot, happy that I got such a close spot. Then, I reach into the back of the car and grab the sign that says, "M. PICKETT."

I'm nervous, and I check myself over in the side mirror one last time. I look put together, which is saying something. Because I definitely don't feel put together.

I feel broken, shattered, and I miss my mother right now. I'm not sure why the grief hit me as I pulled into the airport. But it hit me hard, and it takes me a moment to catch my breath. I don't have time for mental breakdown, not right now.

I walk into the airport, holding my sign. I'm right on time, and I quickly find the arrival gate.

I check my watch when I see people already walking through the security gate. His flight must have arrived early, because I barely have time to show my sign when a man in a well-cut suit catches my eye.

Brown hair with deep set brown eyes, I can tell he's well-built and he fills out his suit. And I find myself staring at him, instead of looking to the crowd for someone who responds to my sign.

The well-built man, he looks at me, and his eyes widen with a nod as he sees my sign.

He walks forward, and my heart tumbles in my chest.

As he reaches me, he holds out his hand.

"Are you Mrs. Grant?"

I reach for him, hoping that I don't embarrass myself.

"Ms.," I say, grasping his warm, large hand. "And you're Mr. Pickett?"

"Michael is fine," he says. He gives me a warm smile, then stands awkwardly in front of me for a few seconds.

"And Regina is fine for me," I say, clearing my throat a little when it cracks.

Pull it together.

"Should we go get my bags?"

"Yeah," I say, snapping myself out of whatever lustful infatuation that's going through my head. I realize that it has been a long time since I've been with a man, which is probably why I'm having such a visceral reaction to him. I need to shake it off, because Michael is here on business.

We don't talk to each other as we wait for his bags, and the next word isn't really uttered until I'm pulling out of the airport.

"How was your flight?"

It's the best I can do right now, the best I can offer.

"It was good, thank you for asking. I was just wondering if you could tell me a bit about what sort of difficulties you're having?"

Business. Michael is here on business. Not for anything else. And I hope that the lurch in my chest every time I look over to him stops sometime.

"I'm having trouble with my mother's estate," I say honestly. The grief comes, hot and fast, and I find myself blinking back tears as I exit onto the freeway. "She did something with the books, and I don't know if I can figure it out."

Michael nods, and he gives me a sympathetic look.

"Are you hungry?"

The question falls out of my mouth, just like the flight question. I really feel that I'm embarrassing myself, but Michael looks over at me with a warm smile.

"I could eat," he says.

"There's a pretty good diner in our town, would you like to head there?"

"Sounds great," he says with a nod.

I spend the rest of the drive to the diner inside awkward silence. Michael looks at the window, at the passing views of Texas and I keep glancing over, trying to catch his eye.

Pull it together, Regina. You're not a schoolgirl.

I pull into the diner, and Michael seems pleased. He smiles at me and gets out of the car.

We sit down in a booth, and I take a look at the menu. It hasn't changed, and I know that I want the burger.

"What's good?" He asks.

"Can't go wrong with a burger and shake here," I answer honestly. "The classic."

"Awesome. I love a good classic."

I smile at him.

"Me too."

The waitress comes over, takes our orders and leaves.

"So, what did your mother do?" Michael asks. He leans forward on the table and seems genuinely interested in what I'm going to say.

"She owned a bakery in town. Owned it for forever, actually." I try not to choke up when I talk about it. Michael sees the emotion in my eyes.

"I'm sorry for your loss. Truly I am. I know it must be very hard."

"She was the rock, you know?" I blurt out, surprised that I'm telling him all this. "She was the anchor. Me and my sisters… well, we don't function well without her."

"You'll learn to," he says, like a man who knows what he is talking about. "There will be a new normal. Life will never be the same, but you'll evolve and change to fit the grief into the day to day."

I nod, appreciative for the support offered by the man I just met.

Our burgers come, along with our shakes. Michael nods his head appreciatively as he takes his first bite.

"Good call," he says with a smile.

I smile back.

"I'm glad you like it."

As soon as the food lands in front of me, my stomach grumbles at the smell. I'm not sure if I remembered to eat today, and internally I give my head a bit of a shake. Sometimes I get so wrapped up in my work that I forget to take care of myself.

I finish my burger, as does Michael. He takes his wallet out and pays while I offer a protest.

"My treat," he says, giving me a warm smile.

"Thank you. I appreciate it."

"I know."

I can't believe how much I like talking to this man about anything. I wait awkwardly by the door before he comes with me back to the car.

"I'll drop you off at your hotel," I say, pulling out of the diner. "And I'll pick you up tomorrow morning."

"Sounds good." He looks at me, dark eyes catching mine. "We'll fix whatever your mother did to those books and keep the bakery open. I promise."

Chapter Six

MICHAEL

I watch her leave and can't quite comprehend the rising anxiety in my chest.

It's like I don't want to be separated from her, which doesn't make any sense, considering I just met the woman. It must be the leftover anxiety of flying.

The hotel is surprisingly clean and well decorated considering where we are and how small this town is.

"Hello," the young woman manning the front desk says as I approach. "Do you have a reservation today?"

"Yes," I say, flipping through my phone to find the confirmation number that Livia sent to me. "For Michael Pickett."

"We've been expecting you," she says with a warm smile. "We don't get a lot of people from out of town here, unless there's a conference."

I don't know what to say to that, so I just give her a warm smile. She busies herself getting my key card ready for me.

"You are in room 204," she says, circling the number at the bottom of the key card folder. "And we now have free Wi-Fi! You don't need a password on anything, just find Quality Inn and click on the Guest access. Should take you right in."

"Thank you," I say, grabbing the packet she passes over to me.

The anxiety in my chest at being separated from Regina doesn't lessen during this encounter, and I'm annoyed more than anything. There's grit behind my eyes as a sudden exhaustion hits me. I need to relax. It must just be stress from the flight.

I'm trying desperately not to think of Regina. She is absolutely gorgeous, and I can't believe how much I enjoyed my ride from the airport. Dark-skinned, piercing dark eyes, and curves in all the right places. I knew I wanted her. As soon as I saw her, I knew it.

And all I wanted to do was get her to pull the car over on the drive to the diner. There were so many places we could have stopped to have some fun, and the entire ride

I looked out the window and imagined what I would do with her. But that was distinctly unprofessional, and I hold myself to the highest standards. I unlock my hotel room door, and step inside. Surprise filters through me again, as I see two neatly made beds in a larger room than anticipated.

I throw my suitcase onto a bed and make my way over to the bathroom.

I hate flying, and I need to get the stink of it off of me. I usually drive to all my appointments, but I knew this was important as soon as Livia approached me with the task.

Pulling my tie loose, I strip off my collared shirt and toss in unceremoniously onto the bed.

The thoughts of Regina consume me, and I hope that the hot water will help me focus. I run it, hotter than usual, fogging up the bathroom. Then I take my jeans off and toss them into the corner of the bathroom. I will be wearing a suit to do business with Regina tomorrow.

I have to keep this professional. It's a favor to a friend, nothing more, and I can't be undressing her with my eyes every time I see her. I step into the shower, allowing the hot water to pelt away the stench of the airplane.

It doesn't matter if she's all legs. With an ass for the gods and breasts that I can't help but notice. I'm here on business. And this teenage infatuation needs to be resolved before I see her tomorrow.

I know that I'm going to be working with her closely for a while, and I can't help but want to get this task over with quickly. I don't want to do anything stupid, especially with a client.

But and I start to soap myself and try to get myself clean, I know that task may prove to be impossible. She's hot. Hotter than any other woman I'd ever seen.

It's not like I don't have experience with hot women. I do. but there is something about Regina Grant, something I can't quite put my finger on. Something that's pulling me in my chest.

I shake my head, redirecting the hot water to pound over top of my shoulders. I'm hoping that my tense shoulders will relax with the hot water.

Unfortunately, the opposite happens, and my head goes to imagining Regina in the shower behind me.

To her long, lithe body pressing up against me. My heart rattles as I imagine her fingertips drifting down my rock-hard abs to-

"Pull it together," I say out loud, snapping my focus back to the present. "That's never going to happen. You're here as a favor. Not to mess around with a client."

I chalk my fantasy up to the mounting exhaustion. It's probably just the flight getting to me. There's no way I'm this attracted to someone, not right after I first met them.

That's impossible. I relax in the shower and can't keep Regina out of my head. Her curvy body, with sky-high legs, rounded hips, full lips, all of it has me shaken to the core.

I'm here on business. I can't forget that. I'm here as a favour to a friend, nothing more. And it wasn't in my contract to use a business trip to get laid. I am always strictly professional.

I wash my hair with the hotel soap, and I'm pleased that it's not terrible quality. It's not like I pamper myself, but I have a standard. And that standard usually means that I bring my own toiletries from home.

Regina weaves her way through my brain again, and this time it's harder to push the thoughts aside.

I may always be strictly professional, but it's never been this hard before.

I can't help but wonder what might happen over the course of the next few days.

As much as it annoys me, I can't help but look forward to seeing her tomorrow morning.

Chapter Seven

REGINA

Today I don't wake up with a pit of dread in my stomach. Instead, the dread is replaced by an almost excited feeling. I'm not exactly sure why- maybe I'm just nervous to have Michael help me with Mama's things. Or maybe I'm excited because of how handsome he looked last night...

I quickly shake that thought out of my head, jump out of bed and into the shower. I throw on one of my typical outfits, glance in the mirror, and stop short. I can't let Michael see me in this- this is hideous. No. Who cares what some man thinks about how I dress? I swipe some nude lipstick over my full lips, grab my purse and head to pick him up.

The Muffin Top happens to be on the way to his hotel, so I stop and get two coffees to go. I'm sure he's going to need it; I know I do- I barely got any sleep last night.

I pull up to the front of the hotel and this man is already standing outside waiting for me. He looks extra tall and lean today in a nice grey suit, briefcase at his side. I can't help but be impressed by his punctuality- very professional, I like it.

As soon as he spots me, he heads to the passenger side. My heart speeds up a little and I have to remind myself to keep breathing. Why am I acting this way? This is so foolish.

His scent immediately envelopes the car as he enters, but not in an overpowering way. It's more sensual, almost like his scent draws me to him, beckoning me to come closer. Before I blurt out something stupid, I hand him his coffee, while taking a huge gulp of mine. I need to stop, this is business. He's here for business.

'Get your head on straight, Regina.'

"So, how did you sleep?" I ask.

'Stupid. Who asks that?!' I silently yell at myself.

"Actually not too great," he responds, seeming to think nothing of it.

'Whew.'

"I'm sorry, jet lag?"

"Not exactly, I think I was just a bit distracted. But don't worry, I'm all ready for today. Thanks for this coffee, this is amazing!"

"You're welcome. It's from my dead mom's bakery."

'*Why did I say that??*'

"Oh that's right, you mentioned the bakery yesterday. Well, her coffee is amazing."

"She didn't make it, my sister did."

"Oh."

'*Why are you acting like this?!*'

We drive the rest of the way to Mama's in silence, but I sneak little glances out of the corner of my eye. As soon as we arrive, I direct us straight to the office.

"Wow, you weren't kidding. This is a mess," Michael states. He isn't wrong.

"Yeah, and this is after months of sorting through everything. I tried cleaning up as much as I could when I heard you were coming, so it didn't totally overwhelm you."

"No, it's okay. This is what I came to do. And trust me, I've seen worse." I know he's lying to make me feel better, and I'm not sure if I like or dislike that.

I gather up all the most important documents, and hand them to him.

"Look over these, and then we can get started," I state.

He takes a seat behind the desk, and I head to the kitchen for a glass of water. I'm not sure why, but my mouth feels unusually dry right now. I down the whole glass before returning to the office and taking a seat across from him.

He seems to be taking his sweet old time looking over each and every document. I guess I should be happy that he's being so precise, but with every minute I just get more and more nervous. I find myself wishing that I had just taken care of this on my own. I don't like watching someone else do the work for me. This is *my* mom's estate; *I* should be the one handling it.

I almost want to rip those papers out of his hands and do it all myself, just to show him I can. I don't want him thinking I'm some damsel in distress. Shaking my head, I realize how stupid I sound. I called him here for a reason, and I need to accept his help. Besides, we never would have met if it weren't for my needing help.

As soon as he's finished, and we begin discussing things- all thoughts of any kind of attraction I had towards him, quickly fade as I begin to take over and micromanage him. What infuriates me even more is that the more I try to help, the more he resists me and does his own thing. Of course, this drives me crazy- because *no one* resists my help. Who does this man think he is??

Every single time I try to voice my opinion on something, he shuts me down almost immediately. What was Livia thinking, sending him here?? I want him *gone*.

We spend the entire rest of the morning arguing over how to handle each and every little thing. We can't agree on a single thing. I'm about ready to kick him out of the damn house when he puts his hand up.

"Regina."

"What."

"You called me here to help- did you not?"

"I mean, technically I called Livia, but-"

"You need help, Regina. That's all I'm here to do. But I haven't even been here for twenty-four hours and you're already not letting me do what I came here for. Now, what I propose is that we just split everything for now, and we can work on our piles separately, Because this right here? This is not productive."

Chills run down my spine at the tone in his voice. The way he handles me… well, I can definitely say that no one has ever had the balls to handle me like this. I can't even begin to describe how much that turns me on.

I nod my head in agreement, unable to open my mouth. No man has *ever* rendered me speechless before.

Chapter Eight

MICHAEL

Today is my first full day in Texas to help Livia's friend, Regina, and I have to say- this is not at all how I expected it to go. The day started off fine- she even brought me some amazing coffee. But then things got weird.

We have been arguing non stop all morning, from the very moment we started working. This woman is quite literally insane- and I don't say that about people often. I have absolutely no idea how I'm going to survive through multiple weeks with her. It's going to be impossible.

Every little thing I suggest, every detail I point out- she instantly shoots it down. Nothing I say is up to par, she always has a different "better" suggestion. My question is- if she isn't going to let me do anything- then why the hell am I here?? And why didn't Livia give me some kind of warning about her?? She's definitely going to hear it from me when I get back home- I don't care if she's my boss *or* that this is her friend.

I don't know whether to be insulted or to just chalk it up to stress from her mother's death- but she's the one who requested this help. If she didn't want it, then what's the point of all this? I didn't volunteer to come here- she *asked* for this. All I want to do is just turn to her and shout all of this. But no, I'm a gentleman.

Although she's going through a particularly rough time in her life- something tells me that her attitude isn't coming from any that. No, something tells me that this is just who she is. Somehow that angers me even more. Who does she think she is?

I finally suggested that we just split things, so we can work separately without any arguing. Reluctantly, she agreed. So now we're sitting on opposite ends of the room, working quietly. Well, *almost* quietly. Every ten minutes or so, she gets up and comes to peek over my shoulder to scoff at what I'm doing, before going back to her stack. I've never met a more infuriating woman.

Despite all of that- I still find her to be the sexiest woman I've ever met- maybe even more so now. Her stubbornness, her confidence, turns me on so much that I have to keep adjusting myself as I work so that she doesn't notice the huge bulge in my pants. The truth is…

all I want to do is throw her down on this table and fuck her until she's screaming my name.

Staying focused on the papers in front of me is proving to be harder than I thought. My eyes keep drifting towards her, and my mind keeps wandering, imagining all the things I would do to her. If only she knew.

The fact that this insane woman turns me on so much that I can't even focus on anything else, makes me a hundred times angrier at her. Is she doing this to me on purpose? Because there's no way she doesn't feel something between us. Seriously, you could cut the sexual tension in this room with even a blunt knife.

She comes over once again to look at what I'm doing. I didn't have time to adjust myself again before she got to me, so there's no way she doesn't see it. I start getting a bit nervous until I realize that I actually want her to see it. The fact that she even has the balls to come over and judge what I'm doing after we agreed to work separately- is so incredibly sexy.

I turn to her, finally having enough.

"Can I help you with something?" I ask.

"Just making sure you aren't fucking anything up," she mutters, scanning my work.

"You know, I don't have to do this at all- I can just go home," I challenge her.

She finally looks at me, shock written across her face.

"I didn't say anything about not wanting you here. Whatever, I'll just stay on my side."

She struts back to her seat, and the sight of her ass moving as she walks makes my bulge even harder. I don't know how much longer I can take this. This is pure torture.

What is it about this woman that has me acting like this? I have *never* been this distracted, tortured, and turned on by anyone- and I've been with some pretty beautiful women. But it's more than looks with Regina, I think. Obviously, she's a stunning woman, and she has an amazing body- but I don't think that's what has me squirming in my chair.

I try to refocus myself back on the papers in front of me, but nothing I'm reading is sticking. None of it is actually sinking in. I'm half tempted to go for a bathroom break and take care of this pent of frustration. And the scent of her that keeps wafting over to me is *especially* not helping. I really need to get myself together, this is insanely unprofessional. This just isn't me.

After a few minutes I get up and head to the bathroom- not to take care of it- but to splash some cold water on my face. This has *got* to stop. I stare at myself in the mirror, splash my face one more time and head back in. I am determined to remain focused- I have to.

Chapter Nine

MICHAEL

I finally get into the swing of things, somewhat. Regina has stopped hovering over my shoulder, and I'm able to move a little more quickly through the stack of papers in front of me. Plus, not looking at her has made it easier for me to tell myself I'm not sitting across from this insanely beautiful woman. Instead, I convince myself that it's a balding middle-aged man that smells like boiled egg.

Regina flips her hair over her shoulder and a sweet floral scent winds its way up my nose into my throat. My attempt at ignoring her immediately ruined. I look up to see she is absentmindedly twisting her gold hoop earring in between her fingers. My slacks start to tighten again.

Damn it. Having to re-adjust on my seat, I reach across the table to pick up a blue ink pen. Luckily, I also find an old newspaper that I can prop on my lap to hide my… swelling.

"Everything okay over there?" I ask. Regina hasn't been this quiet since the moment she picked me up from the airport.

"Fine. It's going fine," she responds.

"Okay, then. I guess we are to pretend everything is *fine.*" I answer back with just as much recoil.

Not convinced by her answer, I try to ignore the tone of disdain in her voice. She is staring at a sun-damaged paper that could pass as being from the '40s. Her eyes dart across the page as I watch a small strand of hair break free from her slicked backed bun.

For a moment, I feel like I am watching her in slow motion. The sun bounces off her rich chocolate hair as she smooths it back down with one hand. Suddenly, the sound of my heartbeat has flooded my ears. I clear my throat and turn my attention back to my own stack of work.

"I can't make this out as a '6' or a '9'?" I think out loud.

"Give it to me," Regina says. "I can read anything in my mother's handwriting."

"It's not the handwriting. Your mother must not have been a very tidy lady. It looks like something spilled on the paper and smeared her writing."

Regina's eyes light up. And not in that cute 'I was just surprised with a gift' way. More of a 'I am going to fly across this desk and strangle you' way.

Shit.

"Of course she was a tidy woman. How could you possibly come to that conclusion from looking at a few tax papers!"

I don't dare to respond. Her glare is still fixed on me, her cheeks flush, and her hands clenched.

"I'm sorry, Regina. I didn't mean it that way. I just- oh, never mind. Forget I said anything."

Regina lowers back into her chair, but her gaze remains unrelenting.

Hello foot, meet mouth.

"You didn't know my mother," Regina said softly. She looks down as she digs her fingernails into the palms of her hands. "She was passionate about everything she did. So what if she got some dough on the paperwork. That doesn't make her a messy person."

I want to tell her I get it, but I don't. Obviously, I didn't mean to say she was messy, I was just commenting on the smudge. Do I even try to fix this? I study Regina's face and her eyes are glistening. Before a tear can fall from the corner of her eye, she turns away from me.

I can still make out the profile of her face. Her jaw quivers as I am sure she is crying now. I see her gently bite down on her lipstick stained lip. I mimic the bite unconsciously. Again, my heart starts to race, and this time I hold my breath as my chest begins to tighten. Her beauty has me captivated, unable to move- and completely unable to look away.

"Are you going to keep working or are you going to just sit there and waste my time," she says. Her sharp tone rips me out of my daydream, and I am quickly reminded of the volatile tension between us.

'This is a job, not a vacation,' I remind myself.

Of course, if it were a vacation, neither of us would have clothes on by this point.

'Focus, get the job done, and then go home. That is all you have to do Michael.'

Maybe I was a little too harsh. She did just lose her mother after all. Was I harsh? I flew all the way out here to 'Mid Town Yee-haw, Texas' just to help her. Shouldn't she be a little nicer to me? After all, this is a favor, and it's not even *my* favor, it's Livia's. I shouldn't be wasting my time on her when I have my own clients to worry about.

Regina lets out a swear as she drops a folder onto the floor. Papers jump into the air then gently float back down to the floor. She climbs off her chair and awkwardly maneuvers in her skirt in an attempt to kneel down without flashing me.

I accidently let out a sympathetic chuckle. Thankfully she doesn't hear it or else I'm sure it would turn into another heated maelstrom of misplaced emotion.

Taking a second to look around the room, I notice the office walls are filled with family photographs. Then I look at Regina. She was still on her knees picking up the papers strewn in a chaotic mess around her. This may be a favor from Livia, but she did promise me that I would be paid. That makes it a job, and I'll do anything to make sure the job gets done.

I turn my chair to the side so Regina is out of my direct line of sight. If I can't see her, I won't get as distracted, right? I pick up another pile of papers and let them fall firmly onto the desk in front of me.

Whatever it takes.

Chapter Ten

MICHAEL

"So, no?" I ask. Right now, the only thing I'm trying not to do is curse. A lot. My pen is hovering over one of the sheets in the paperwork of Regina's mother's real estate stuff. The date on this page is smudged a bit — ruined ink — and I think it says 2008, but I can't be sure. Regina claims she can read everything, so I'm trying to ask her, but she feels the need to have some thirty second delay to every question I ask.

"Hm?" she asks, glancing at me. Her eyebrows are furrowed, focused on her own page. She won't even look up at me all the way.

"Regina."

"What?"

"So this is or isn't 2008?" I point to the page again.

"Let me see."

"I just showed you— fine." I pass the paper over to her.

"It's 2008."

"That's what I was asking. Thank you." I move to take the paper back, but then she pulls it closer to herself.

"What is this?"

"It's a 530. Let me see it again."

"Are you sure?"

"Am I sure about what? The 2008? 'Cause I'm—"

"No, are you sure that it's a 530. How do you know?"

"Yes, I'm sure. I've been doing this forever. Just hand it back."

Ignoring me, she begins scanning the page. There is a lot to go through, so I can see how Regina couldn't handle all of this alone and needed to call Livia, but I know for a fact it would go faster if she would work with me instead of acting like I'm the enemy here.

I didn't fly out to El Paso to be butting heads with some former financial firm exec. I just want to get in, get things done, and then leave, which is the same thing I have done with every other case before hers. And sure, I've dealt with difficult clients but none as difficult as Regina.

"Regina, could you please hand it back?"

"Fine, fine," she says, handing it back to me finally. "You don't have to be so snippy about everything, you know."

"I'm not being snippy. I just wanted it back, so I can finally get it done. We've been here for three hours already, and we haven't made nearly as much progress as we should." I take the paper and set it on the table again.

"You're the only thing taking a while here. I'm moving faster."

"This isn't a race."

"Only because you're losing." She smirks. "And why are you using a blue pen instead of a black one?" she asks me. Why she's asking this now when I've been using exclusively blue pens since we started is a mystery to me. She's so nitpicky. And yet people call me the uptight one.

"Blue pen is easier to read and distinguish from the rest of forms. Plus, it's better for memory, though that's unrelated."

"Black's more professional."

"Blue is best to use. There's basically a consensus that it's better."

"Obviously not, since I've been using black. Black is better."

"Are we really going to do this now?" It's so insignificant.

"My mom always used black pen, too. You'll see it right on these forms."

"Yes, on these nearly illegible forms." I'll admit the last comment may be a bit too far, but she's getting on my last nerve at this point. Why does she have to make everything so hard?

"These aren't illegible." By the way she's scooting her chair back, I can tell I've hit yet another nerve with her. I understand that her mother died. I also understand that this means she is having to deal with the woman's death along with all of this confusing real estate law stuff.

And it's not that I'm not trying to be understanding- of course I am- but I'm equipped to deal with property law, not the whirlwind of emotions that Regina is.

I went to law school for a career and to learn about essential things. And nowhere was there a class all about the vicissitudes of Regina Grant. So where am I supposed to go from here when she is the only difficult part about this?

Her feelings are hurt, and it's not that I don't care or something, but I just don't know what to do about it. If I did, maybe we wouldn't be having so much trouble right now. Sighing, I prepare myself for the lecture bubbling in her.

"The words are perfectly legible. Maybe you just can't read. I'll admit things aren't as neat as some of your big businesses, but my mother didn't have a million accountants. She was a small business owner, but more than that, she just loved to bake.

The other stuff mattered more than the books. She did run an honest business, though, so maybe you should just put your head down and work on getting things organized instead of complaining about a few measly numbers *you* can't read."

"Look, I'm sorry, okay? Will you just give me the paper back?"

She shoves it back at me.

I'm handling this the way I handle all of my cases. Maybe if she didn't take everything personally, this wouldn't be so hard. I've dealt with messy and old handwriting before, but I guess I usually deal with the employees of the business owners, not their children. Nothing could have prepared me for this.

Regina is giving me a sharp glare now.

"Hey, I have an idea," I say.

"What?" she asks.

"Would you be able to take me to get a rental car?" I don't mention that the reason for this is to avoid having to rely on her for everything, but I'm sure she gets it.

"First good idea you've had," she says, already standing. "I'll get my purse and we can go." I'm sure what she's not saying is that this way she won't have to be around me all the time. Either way, it's a win-win for both of us.

"Great." I leave the paper and stand as well. Maybe things will get better from here (or maybe not).

Chapter Eleven

REGINA

After my whirlwind of a day with Michael arguing over the estate, I decide to visit Bridgid at the bakery for some much-needed sweets. I really just don't want to be at the house after all the arguing that I did there today. At least Michael has a rental car now, so I don't have to drive him to and from his hotel every day, but god that man is a *dick*.

"To what do I owe this pleasure?" Bridgid says when she sees me walk in.

I plop down at a table, sighing.

"Today was exhausting, girl. I don't know if I can work with this man. He literally just wants to control everything and it's fucking infuriating."

Bridgid lifts one eyebrow and gives me her look.

"I know, I know. It's my payback for doing that to you all these years. But my mother just died for god's sake, you think he'd be a little more sensitive."

"Well, Reggie, maybe he isn't trying to offend you. Maybe you're just taking everything the wrong way because you're extra sensitive about Mama."

"I don't know, he's pretty condescending. He doesn't strike me as someone who doesn't know what he's doing. I think he's acting this way on purpose."

"Yeah, but Reg, why would he do that? He doesn't even know you. What motive would he possibly have?"

"I don't know B, he's just an ass. Some people are just like that."

"Well, the way I see it you don't really have an option but to coexist with him. You hired him, so unless you're gonna send him back to Chicago and go at this alone- you're gonna have to just get over this grudge you have against him."

"I guess."

"Hey, I know- why don't we go out tonight? You need to get your mind off of all this shit. Let's go to the bar, me, you and Joel!!"

"Ehh, I don't know. I don't really feel like being a third wheel all night."

"Oh come on, you're not going to be a third wheel, we're sisters, that's impossible. Besides, it'll be a chance for you and Joel to spend some more time together. I love seeing you guys get to know one another. He likes you."

"Ugh, *fine*. But only because getting drunk sounds *perfect* to me after the day I just had. I'll go home and change and then you guys can meet me at the house once you're closed up and ready?"

"Sounds good! See ya then!"

I grab a cupcake and head out the door. I'm actually happy that she suggested this. I think it'll be good for me. And I really just need some alcohol in my system.

Once home I change into a strapless black dress, throw on some jewelry and some makeup, and leave my hair loose and curly. I swipe some of my favorite red lipstick on and I'm ready to go.

We decide to meet at the bar instead of Mama's, so I head there a little early to do some pregaming. Tonight will be my night to just relax and let loose- which I haven't allowed myself to do in a loong time. I take two shots of whiskey before they even arrive.

"Heeeeey!" I greet them, obviously already buzzed.

"Woah, someone already started!" Joel says.

"I sure did ya west coast boy!"

"Oh god, it's gonna be one of those nights, isn't it? Why don't we order some bar food, so you don't get completely smashed, huh? You probably haven't eaten all day"

"Just the cupcake I stole from you before I left the bakery!"

We order some fries and a basket of chicken tenders. I devour it all, and they end up ordering more for themselves. I guess I didn't realize how hungry I was until they brought the food to our table.

"I like seeing you enjoy yourself Reg. You've been so stressed lately- we need to take you out like this more often. You deserve it you know."

"I know, it's just hard with everything. I mean Mama aside, what the fuck am I doing? I don't even have a job, B," I whimper, burying my face in my hands.

"Oh come on, don't act like you don't deserve a little time off. You've worked your ass off your entire life. You're due for a bit of a resting stage. Besides, it's not like you're not doing anything- you've been working nonstop since you got here."

"I know, I know," I say, flagging the bartender over so I can order another drink.

I'm actually surprisingly enjoying myself. The food is good, drinks are good, music is good. Even the conversation between the three of us is flowing well. It really starts to feel like a fun night out. I almost forgot what that even felt like.

After a few beers, Joel decides he wants to show us some of his "dance moves", which only cause us to die in a fit of laughter together. I actually quite like him, especially for my sister. They really are perfect together, and I find it so beautiful that they found each other during such a horrible time in her life. It really was such a blessing and I'm so happy for both of them.

After a couple of hours, I find myself feeling relaxed and actually having fun. I haven't thought about Michael or the estate the entire time. I haven't even thought about Mama. This whole night out thing is turning into a wonderful idea. I decide that I need to spend some more time with Bridgid like this, I think it would be good for both of us.

I love the way the two of us have been getting along lately. Sure, there's the occasional sarcastic remark- but nothing compared to how it was just a few months ago. It feels good, like we're reconnecting after all this time. I know Mama would be so proud to see us like this.

Chapter Twelve

MICHAEL

It's not until I've got my drink in hand – a local rye whiskey, neat – that I turn myself around on my bar stool and check out the restaurant. Not ten seconds into my panoramic scan, I come up short.

A particular table has caught my eye. It's got three occupants. I don't know the guy and girl who are facing my direction. But, even in the dimly lit bar, I definitely recognize the one with her back to me. Seeing Regina makes me freeze with my drink halfway to my lips.

Of course she's here. It's a small town. The odds of us both ending up in the same place for a drink aren't that astronomical. It still feels like more than a coincidence, which is stupid, because I'm not the kind of person to believe in fate. At least, I don't think I am- I never have been before.

I would expect that discovering her here would put a damper on my mood. After all, didn't I come out to the bar to put her craziness out of my mind? So why am I finding myself hopping off my barstool and heading toward her table?

I spend the ten seconds it takes me to get across the bar trying to second guess myself. To come up with a reason why this is a bad idea. The problem is that even from behind and seated, there is something magnetic about Regina. Something about the way she's lounging makes me jealous of the chair. Makes me wish the bar were completely empty and I could pull her out of that seat and into my arms –

Then I realize I'm at the table, standing directly behind Regina, and the guy and girl I don't know are staring up at me with raised brows.

The woman has a similar complexion and build to Regina. My guess is that she's one of the sisters. Probably the youngest one, given the way she's leaning into that white guy, who I assume is the new beau I've heard about.

We all know that the way to a man's heart is through his stomach. Less widely known is that sometimes the way to a woman's is through her siblings. Time to dive in.

"Hello," I announce and tip my glass to them.

Regina, directly in front of me, stiffens. I glance down. She's wearing a sleeveless top and I can see the skin of her shoulders ripple across with goose bumps. Nice to know that I make an impression.

The one I assume is the sister notices Regina's sudden stiffness, as well. A flash of intrigue lights in her eyes. She looks up at me.

"I'm Michael Pickett," I say to her, "I'm here helping Regina with –"

"Mama's finances," she finishes. I was right, it *is* one of the sisters. Knew it. And from her smile, my guess is that she's the sweet one Regina told me about.

"Let me guess," I say, "Bridgid?"

"Good guess. And this is my husband, Joel."

The guy half-rises from his chair and we shake. I extend a hand to Bridgid, as well. "Funnily enough, we've heard a lot about you," she says, taking it.

"That must be why my ears were burning."

"Want to join us?"

Regina stiffens even more at her sister's invitation. I can't see her face, but I can imagine her eyes are trying to send a signal on the order of 'no' to '*hell* no'.

Maybe that's partly why I say, "Yes, I would love to."

I settle into the chair beside Regina. Her groan does not go unnoticed by me. I ignore it and put all my attention on the other two.

Joel leans forward and points the neck of his beer in my direction. "You be thorough with all that paperwork. That bakery means everything to this family."

"I've gotten that impression. And what a family it is."

"I hate to break this to you, but the sweetest and prettiest one is already spoken for." He squeezes Bridgid a little closer to him. She kisses his cheek. Young love can be so cheesy.

"Noted," I say somberly.

Bridgid leaps into the conversation with a canny smile, saying, "Oh, Joel, I'm sure Michael's got plenty of admirers back in Chicago."

Out of the corner of my eye, I try to see if that comment elicits any response from Regina. She remains as still as Lake Michigan on a windless day. I throw my attention back onto Bridgid.

"Work tends to keep me from too much socializing, actually."

"Oh no. Another type-A…"

The talk of relationships starts to make me uncomfortable. I wonder if I've made a mistake, not pulling the ripcord before I sat down. I turn my attention to Joel. "So, you're in the mortuary business, huh?"

"Yeah. No jokes, please."

"I don't joke about how anyone chooses to make a living. Besides, it's a noble profession."

"Hey, I like this guy," Joel announces to the group. Then he turns back to me. "Wait a second, are you a White Sox fan?"

"Cubs."

"Then we can be friends. I'm an A's fan. Originally from the Bay Area. If you're a National League guy, though, there's no rivalry between us."

"Unless we both end up in the World Series."

"In which case hell would have frozen over."

I smile. He's a good guy. The next twenty minutes end up being a lot of talk about sports and work. Joel turns out to be a numbers wonk, like me, so we go back and forth from discussing different players stats to the viability of different small business models.

Bridgid, clearly still in the flush of early love, seems enraptured by Joel's enthusiasm for any topic or bit of minutiae. Must be nice to have someone in your life who thinks so highly of you at all times.

Must also be kind of boring.

As Joel and I talk, with Bridgid throwing in the occasional comment, Regina stays deathly quiet. She just stares into her drink like she wishes she could trade places with it. We've all ordered another round before she's even halfway through the one she had when I sat down.

A part of me enjoys making her a little bit miserable, given the way she's been driving me up a wall.

A bigger part of me hopes that when the night is over, Bridgid and Joel might become my advocates in all things Regina-related.

Chapter Thirteen

REGINA

The second Michael shows up at our table, everything goes sideways. What was he doing here? It wasn't bad enough he had to drive me crazy all day, now he wanted to intrude upon my night out?

What's worse is watching Bridgid and Joel happily chat with the guy. Can't they see what a hard-nosed, narrow-minded, judgmental jerk he is? Exhibit A: look at the way Michael plopped himself down at the table and immediately hijacked the conversation.

There's no denying that hearing his voice sent a wave of feeling through me that had more going on than just irritation. Oh, irritation is a big part of it, no doubt… but I don't really feel like exploring the rest of the feeling.

So I sit there and nurse my drink and try to not engage. I wait for Bridgid to notice that I am displeased with the situation. She notices alright… but just keeps grinning and chuckling, enjoying Joel and Michael.

I finally toss back the rest of my drink. I'm debating getting another one, when Michael shifts in his seat, gesturing wildly about whatever sports thing he and Joel are discussing. In shifting, his knee brushes mine. I feel a flutter that starts in my thighs, shoots between my legs and ends at my breasts.

That's it.

"OK, I'm out," I announce, shooting straight out of my chair.

Bridgid looks a little guilty. Too bad it's too little too late. "No, sis, stay, c'mon," she pleads.

"We're having a great time," Joel says.

"The night is still young," Michael adds.

"Nope. I'm beat. See ya." I reach into my purse, throw a few bucks on the table, and leave before anyone can protest.

As I drive back to the house, I try to tell myself I'm not upset. When I realize my foot is being quite heavy on the gas, I ease it up and try to drive just like a person who is totally cool with everything going on in her life. I even crank on the radio.

Bad idea. The song coming out of the speakers is by Donovan's favorite artist. Hearing it is like getting sucker-punched in the heart.

I quickly click the radio off and drive the rest of the way back to the house in silence. The house is quiet, too, when I get in and hurry into my childhood bedroom. I close the door behind me and quickly strip out of my clothes and into some sweats.

The best thing for me is bed and sleep. Too bad I'm wide awake, even if my body feels like it's dragging a thousand pounds. It's felt that way since I left Minneapolis.

So I sit on my old bed clutching a pillow and I try to take some comfort in my familiar surroundings. I try to connect with the happy girl who became a mature, driven young woman in this very bedroom.

Except all I feel is alone. All I feel is the failure that's stuck me here with my tail between my legs. If the girl who dreamed big dreams in this room could see me now, she'd be horrified.

How did I get here? Just a few weeks ago, I'd had it all, like Whitney sang. The youngest person ever to be made an executive director at my company. Not to mention the first black woman. It was my dream job, with a clear trajectory that would carry me through to a comfortable retirement somewhere in my late fifties.

Then came the merger. A merger that had become possible partly because of how much I'd helped grow the firm. That didn't matter when the new executive called me into his office. Gave me the old line about the competing office cultures, job redundancies and a lot of other corporate double-talk that finally ended with me being terminated.

You wouldn't believe how quickly all my girlfriends and colleagues left me, then. I thought we'd had relationships built on mutual respect and care. Turned out that was some bullshit. We'd had friendships based on *transactions*. I was just a commodity to them, to be used, bought – and sold when the investment was no longer working.

Through that downward spiral, the one thing I thought I could still rely on was my boyfriend, Donovan.

A short, angry laugh escapes me as I clutch my pillow tighter. The laugh is followed by that ache in my stomach that comes whenever I think about him.

Donovan was handsome, chiseled, with creamy, dark chocolate skin, lips I could kiss for days, and a sleek, shaved head that always felt so right beside me on the pillows at night.

We'd had this supernova, incandescent kind of love. We were the relationship that everyone was jealous of. When the single girls I knew would complain about some date they'd just had, they'd always then sigh and say, "Wish I could have something like you got with Donovan."

Except it turned out what I had with Donovan was bullshit, too. He'd been cheating on me for months. Once I lost my job, and my attention wasn't always on work, the signs of his infidelity became so obvious. I don't know what was more insulting, the cheating or the sloppy way he went about it.

When I confronted him, he didn't even offer excuses or claim he wanted to fix things between us. He basically just shrugged and packed his bags. Tossed me away just like everyone else had.

I drift onto my side on the bed, curled up with the pillow, and wishing Mama was here to hug me again. It's been so long since I was vulnerable, even to myself. I was stoic when I lost the job. Implacable when my friends fled from me. Stony when Donovan's cheating ass went out the door.

But now, I let myself cry. I sob into the pillow. A year's worth of tears, hurt and rage pours out of me.

That's when I remember what Whitney actually sang: 'Didn't we *almost* have it all'.

I fall asleep with a very damp pillow and a very empty heart.

Chapter Fourteen

MICHAEL

"So, you like working for Livia? She and Regina go way back, you know," Bridgid says, bouncing right back from Regina's abrupt exit. It seems Bridgid is the loser of the two, either that or Regina is that ticked off at me. At this point, I don't know which one seems more likely.

"Yeah, Livia's nice, and the office is great. We get things done," I answer, nodding. I am starting to wonder if I should have left. Bridgid had invited me to sit, but the entire time Regina had been sitting there as if she had something up her dress or something. She had barely looked at me once and hit my shoulder on the way out, not that either of us said anything about it.

Sure, Regina and I probably have a little bad blood now, but I'm starting to feel as if it is flowing more from her side than mine. I mean, sure doing all this paperwork with her— and the difficulties that come with that— is hard, but it's not like my negative feelings towards her span beyond that.

I've been here for the past few days to help, and all she's done is resist it at every turn, as if she could do it herself or something. Why did she even call Livia to send me down if she didn't want the help? Sometimes, I have half the mind to just leave and fly back to Chicago and let her figure things out herself- make her wait until Livia can fly down.

Needless to say, things have been exhausting. Honestly, this little reprieve at the bar with Bridgid and Joel is nice. The conversation flows smoothly, no one gets hurt over assumed implications, I don't have to do the whole touchy-feely thing, and now that Regina's gone, there's no tension either. I feel myself relaxing in my seat more and more as the time goes on.

Now, I'll be the first to admit I'm not the most apt when it comes to emotions, but I also doubt I'm nearly as bad as Regina is trying to make me out to be. Half of the time, it seems as if she purposefully misunderstands things and takes my most impersonal comments personally.

She's the one being cold. As I look back up at Bridgid and Joel, I realize I might be starting to get a little obsessive about Regina. After all, I'm in a conversation with two people other than her, but all I can think about is our interactions. Maybe it's a sign of something, but I'm not going to dig anymore into it now.

"Regina seems stressed," Bridgid says, meeting my eyes. I'm not sure if she's saying this to ask me something or to warn me to be a little nicer, but it isn't as if I haven't tried. "Don't you think?" she asks.

"I mean, I guess," I say. I don't know Regina all that personally, and I feel like that question requires me to.

"Do you guys talk while you work?"

"Um, a little, why?" I feel myself growing uncomfortable, so I try not to tense up.

"I don't know... I feel like she's not telling me everything she's feeling right now, you know? It's not just our mother's death. She lost her job, her friends, her boyfriend. There's more going on there than she cares to admit, I think. I thought maybe she might open up to you since she knows how I can be about things... And you seem practical, you know..." She trails off.

"What she means to say is that Bridgid is very caring, and sometimes Regina wants to talk without talking about her feelings. Since you guys don't know each other all that well and you're a bit more… She thinks Regina may say more to you."

"Are you saying I'm cold?" I ask.

"Not exactly," Bridgid cuts in, grinning.

I smile as well.

"I just mean you're less touchy feely."

"Well, that I am," I admit. It's interesting how they danced around it, though.

"Yeah, so if she does say something, and you think maybe I should know, I'd appreciate that," Bridgid finally says. She then holds her hand out. "Here, let me put my number in your phone."

"Sure." I hand it over to her.

"Bridgid is ever the caring sister," Joel chuckles.

"Of course."

"Feel free to call or text anytime." Bridgid hands the phone back to me.

"Cool, I will." I sigh. "Well, I think I should get going soon. We have more paperwork to get to tomorrow, and I think we're both hoping to make some bigger progress. Thanks for your hospitality."

"Hopefully, we'll see you soon," Bridgid says, bidding me goodbye.

"Yeah, hopefully." I mutter the last part as I break away from the counter and head out of the bar. That had been nice, but I need to get back to the hotel and try to get some sleep. I know I'm definitely going to need it.

As I drive back to the hotel, I can't help but feel some draw to this quiet little town. I think I have always dreamed of living somewhere where everyone knew your name and things were small and quaint. It's all definitely a much different place from the one I grew up in.

I went to college, of course, but then I returned to Chicago, as it is the only place I have ever known as home. But this little town makes me think that maybe I could find somewhere else to feel that way.

Soon I'm making my way up to my room. After a quick shower and setting my clothes out for tomorrow, I sit on the side of my bed. I turn my alarm on, and then I'm looking at my text messages. My thumb hovers over Regina's name. I press it quickly:

Had a nice time tonight and enjoyed meeting your family.

I send it off before I can think twice.

Chapter Fifteen

REGINA

"Is this about last night?" Michael has the nerve to ask me.

"Is *what* about last night?"

"Are you being like this because of last night?"

We're back at work on Mama's finances. For the last hour, we managed to be pleasant. By which I mean, we managed to civilly ignore each other. He did his work. I did mine. It was actually… pleasant.

I was feeling refreshed, on top of it all. After my cry last night, I managed to sleep like a baby. A deeper, more invigorating sleep than I've had since I lost my job. Maybe even before that. As I got ready for the day, I even felt ready to deal with Michael. Ideally, we could get things wrapped up quickly and he'd be gone and out of my life.

Instead, he had to bring his attitude… again.

"First of all," I say, turning fully to him so as to engage this latest assault, "I'm not sure what I'm 'being like'."

"Like you – never mind." He tries to drop it. No way I'm letting him off that easy.

"And *second* of all," I continue, "this has nothing to do with last night, it has to do with the fact that you're being condescending."

"How is asking a question about something related to the very important paperwork I'm doing right now in any way 'condescending'?"

"It's the tone."

"Tone?"

"And you know it."

He works his jaw, trying to figure out how to respond to that. Instead, he grits his teeth and turns back to the forms in front of him. The fact that he disengages drives me even more crazy.

Only problem is, I can't figure out in what *way* he makes me crazy. Like, he makes me crazy enough to want to strangle him. I have a brief cartoon fantasy of murdering him, folding his body up, and putting it in the trash bin outside.

But he also makes me crazy enough to want to hop on him and ride him right there where he's sitting. I have a brief, very vivid, much more real fantasy about that, too.

My skin gets warm. I know I ought to turn back to my own work. The sooner I finish my stack of papers, the sooner we can be done. But instead of doing the sensible thing, I stay on him. "Well?" I ask.

"Well what?" he asks back without looking up.

"Do you want an answer to your question?"

"I don't even remember what it was, so no."

"Fine."

I turn myself back to my own work. Except I still feel flush. I still feel that boiling emotion inside me that is sending competing messages to my body: equal parts 'fuck' and 'fight'.

Apparently, he can't manage to focus either. He swivels in his chair to face me again and says, "Y'know, there was nothing in my tone. Forgive me if I'm trying to be professional here."

"Oh, no, *I'm* sorry," I say, laying the sarcasm on thick so even a bonehead like him won't miss it. "I didn't realize that 'professionalism' and 'respect' were mutually exclusive."

"You're one to talk," he says. It seems like he's smiling in spite of himself. It's a handsome smile.

Dammit, I want to stay mad at him. Not be charmed.

"So I'm not respectful?" I ask. I know I'm being difficult. There's something delicious about driving him nuts, though. Something kind of… all right, I'll admit it: sexy.

He throws his arms up in the air. I hate myself for noticing how impressive his shoulders and biceps are.

"I'm just trying to do the job that *you* hired me to do," he says. "Asking questions is part of the job. I'm sorry if you don't like where those questions are going, but every business decision someone makes doesn't somehow automatically turn saintly just because she dies."

The quiet in the room would make the ghosts in a cemetery uncomfortable. The temperature seems to drop about ten degrees. The heat in my body is gone.

"Fuck," he mutters, "I'm sorry, that was."

I take a shallow breath. "Yes, it was."

"I'm —"

"For your information, my Mama *was* a saint. I'm talking about when she was *living*."

"I know."

"So just remember that I *am* the one who hired you and the deceased woman who's finances you're poring over so 'professionally' was my *mother*."

He stands up and looks truly guilty. "Okay… I'm sorry, that was shitty. In my defense, though –"

"Oh, this should be good," I interrupt, and sit back with my arms folded.

"In my defense," he starts again, "it's hard to do this work accurately when I'm constantly walking on eggshells. The fact of the matter is, there are mistakes in the paperwork, some of it is sloppy, and we need to acknowledge that."

"You arrogant, elitist –"

"Just because she ran a small business doesn't mean it didn't have to follow the rules –"

"You are a son-of-a-bitch, you know that."

"Well – you're a hypocrite," he blurts out.

"Excuse me?"

"You talk about being professional and by-the-book, but anytime I bring up the most minute flaw in your mother's accounting, you pounce on me."

"She's my *mother*," I declare, standing up.

"Which is why I want to make sure I get this right," he says inching toward me.

"You just want to throw your superiority in my face," I rebut, inching a little toward him.

"I have no idea what you're even talking about."

"You have no respect for me."

"I have *tons* of respect for you." We're nearly nose-to-nose…

"Is that why you decided to sabotage my evening last night?"

"So this *is* about last night."

"This is about you being the latest worst thing that's happened to me in a long string of recent worst things."

We're so close our noses are nearly touching and I know I have to get out of there. Without thinking, I grab my jacket and storm out of the house. It's not until I'm safely outside that I allow myself to take a deep breath. I shed the tension and shake my arms out.

That was close.

If I stayed in that house any longer, I definitely would have kissed him.

Chapter Sixteen

Wow. That was monumentally stupid.

The front door slams as Regina storms off, pissed at me. And probably rightfully so. Why the hell did I engage like that? And what was up with that crack about her mom.

I start to pursue but get halfway to the front door before I come up short. Engaging her again won't help. Best to let tensions cool and pray she can be professional again in a little bit.

Pray she *can be professional,* I think. *You were hardly the model of workplace appropriateness yourself.*

It's just that she drives me crazy. This is the problem with people. They're so… *interactive.*

Numbers are numbers. They sit there and let you come to them. They have no agenda. They simply are there to tell a story, and that story is always honest and straightforward. So you deal with the truth and you make them make sense.

Which you can do if you know how numbers work. That's my job. And I'm good at knowing numbers and I'm great at making them do what they inherently want to do.

People, less so. And Regina, clearly, not at all.

Why couldn't she understand that all I wanted was to make her mother's numbers literally add up? Why did she have to be so aggressive?

And why the hell did she drive me so nuts?

I couldn't help it. Even as we were trading barbs, it was all I could do not to plant my hands on her sexy hips and pull her into me. She was insulting me, and I was craving her touch. She was ripping me a new one and I was just longing to taste her perfectly full lips.

Even now, still smarting from the fight and still rueing things I'd said, I can almost imagine how she'd feel in my arms. How our bodies would go together, naked, pressed against one another in a passionate embrace, my hands sliding along her…

Whoa, boy. I shake my head and find that I'm holding my breath. And growing an erection despite my wanting to not be interested in Regina. The body is another thing not like numbers. It never listens to reason.

I ignore the remaining paperwork and hurry to the bathroom. I splash some cold water on my face. I briefly debate taking a cold shower to settle my blood pressure and get my guy to stand down. Fortunately, my body comes to its senses on its own. I sigh as the erotic hunger dissipates.

My obsession seems to linger. I keep picturing Regina storming out of the house. I can't help but remember the way her ass swayed as she –

Stop it.

I am not normally an irrational person. Never in my life has a woman knocked me off kilter. It's not that I haven't been in love before. I have. I'm pretty sure I have. I mean, I *definitely* have.

Most recently, for example, there was Alexa. She and I dated for six months a few years ago. She'd told me two months into our relationship that she loved me. And I'd said it back. Which must mean that I was in love. I wouldn't say it otherwise. But instead of love, what we ended up with was bitterness.

The more she said she loved me, and the more I said it back, the more she accused me of working too much.

Caring about my job more than her. Being unfeeling. She said that I was impossible to get through to.

"Then what are you doing with me?" I asked her, finally.

She admitted that she didn't know. The relationship ended right then and there. She cried. I tried to muster some grief as well, so she wouldn't feel embarrassed. And I did genuinely feel bad that she felt bad. I even missed her for a little while.

But there was work to be done at my job. There were financial problems that needed solutions. So I worked and I solved and in time there was no emptiness or sadness or pain where Alexa had been. No void.

That's how my relationships with women have always gone.

Something is definitely different with Regina. Her absence from the house seems palpable to me. Like a part of me just stormed out, too. Which is ridiculous.

No one has ever distracted me like this, before. No one has ever been able to get me to obsess over them before. No one has ever been the last thing I thought about when I was falling asleep. No one has ever made me press against a pillow wishing it was their body.

No one has ever made me want them as badly as I want Regina.

I towel off my face. I force myself back to the table with all of her Mama's paperwork. I feel a deep pang of regret over the comments I made. I realize that no one's ever made me lose my temper like this either. Didn't some poet say there was a fine line between love and hate?

Love and hate? Are you out of your mind? I ask myself. *You just met her. You're being ridiculous. Stop embarrassing yourself.*

I shake my head before staring at the mound of paperwork. Sitting back down, I dive back into it. The work goes slowly, though. It doesn't make any sense, but the curve of every number seems to remind me of the curves of Regina's body.

I redouble my assault on the forms. I remind myself that I'm just here to do a job. That once it's done, I won't have to look at Regina anymore. I won't have to stare at her gorgeous face, or her luscious lips. I won't be in a position to crave her skin and her lips…

Oh, boy. I seriously need to get through this as quickly as possible so that I can get back in my rental car, drop it off, get on a plane, and get back home to Chicago.

Where I can screw my head back on correctly.

Chapter Seventeen

REGINA

By the time I finish walking around the block, my heart and my breathing are back to a semi-normal pace. My mind feels at least somewhat settled. My boiling anger toward Michael has dipped to a light simmer. Truth is, he would deserve it if I threw him out on his ass and drop-kicked him back to Chicago.

In fact, as I was walking, I rehearsed about ten different speeches I could deliver to give him a piece of my mind. Some of them were pretty fierce, too. I am woman, hear me roar level shit.

The quick pace of my walk quickly cooled those feelings. Instead, the lectures quickly gave way, against my will, to daydreams. Some people might call them fantasies. I was not quite willing to go that far. I'll just say that in them, the piece I was giving Michael was not of my *mind…*

Eventually, the walk helped me exorcise those demonic ideas, too. I was able to think clearly. Remind myself that Michael was here for a job and that was it. When the job was done, he would leave.

While I would stay here and lick my wounds.

See that, Regina? When you keep things simple, it's all very clear.

Coming back to the house, I catch a hazy reflection of myself in the window and take a moment to straighten up. Then I fix my face and set my spine up nice and tall before marching back inside.

He doesn't look up as I stride into the office. That's good. He should be hard at work. Just like I am about to be.

I sit myself down without a word. Lose myself in the things that need to get reviewed.

Or at least I try to. Michael is incredibly distracting. How is it possible that every time he moves, I'm aware of it? Each stroke of his pen. Each little shift in his chair. Like I'm programmed to respond to his every muscle twitch. When he clears his throat a little, I have to fight the urge to perk up, expectantly, like I was sure he was about to wax poetic at me.

I try to remind myself that I'm mad at him. But somehow this office has become a pressure cooker of my own unhinged desire. Being so close to him feels like being near an open flame, and I'm getting scorched. Or it's like being near a blanket alive with static electricity, and I keep getting shocked.

It's enough to make a girl's head spin. And mine does.

I go back to reading the document in front of me. The words seem strangely familiar. Oh yeah. That's because it's my fifth attempt at reading this thing. Every time I get three sentences into the legalese, Michael shifts in his seat or flips a page and I'm distracted all over again. How many hours has it taken me to get through just a few paragraphs?

My stomach growls before I even realize I'm hungry. In the completely quiet house, it sounds like a dragon's just come to life.

I freeze. Maybe he'll just ignore it. I glance at him out of the corner of my eye. He's still scribbling something, head down. Whew. That's good. Dodged a bullet the--

"That literally scared me," he mumbles, still involved in his work. "I thought we were under attack for a second."

He turns to me slightly and gives me a half-grin that makes my knees go mushy.

"I'm sorry," I say as flatly as I can. "I'm just hungry." I try to get back to work.

"*You're* hungry," he says, putting down his pen and stretching. "I've been starving since you got back to the house. My stomach finally quit growling and just resigned itself to going to bed with no dinner."

"Why didn't you get yourself something?"

"Are you kidding? I was terrified if my ass moved from this desk, you'd launch into me for not working."

"I would never do that," I protest. Then we lock eyes. "Yeah, I would totally do that," I admit.

We share a laugh. His smile is kind of shy. Like he's uncomfortable showing all his teeth or something. It's sort of adorable. If he weren't a jerk, I'd even go so far as to say it's attractive.

My stomach growls again. I put a hand over my belly and make a face. *Why is my body embarrassing me in front of* this *man of all people?*

"Geez," he says, "you better feed that thing." He points at my belly, glancing at it. Then – or is it my imagination? – his eyes quickly scope out my whole body before self-consciously landing back on my eyes.

I consider him for a moment. Then I offer, "Yeah, why don't we both table this work for the night?"

"You mean I'm off the clock?"

"Punch out, kid."

"Dinner, here I come," he says, quickly starting to rise.

"Why don't I cook us dinner here?"

The words linger in the air of the office a moment, like they aren't sure I really meant to say them. Because I'm not sure I did. They just sort of shot out of me.

Michael is standing half out of his chair, looking like he's not sure he was supposed to have heard what I said. "You… sure?"

Play it off, girl, I tell myself. I stand and shrug like it's no big deal. "Sure. We're both starving. If we go out, there's going to be the time of getting to the place, the wait for a table, the wait to order and be served…"

"We'll be emaciated by then," he jokes.

"Wasted away."

"All right. I'll hang out."

"Good."

I hop out of my seat and move quickly out of the office and toward the kitchen.

"Wait," Michael says, following me, "can you really cook?"

"I can also really poison your food," I point out.

"Truce, truce," he laughs, his hands up.

"Uh-huh. Just for that, you're doing the dishes after."

"Completely earned," he says and follows me to the kitchen.

Prepping the items for dinner gives me an excuse to not look at him. That is a very good thing. Because for some damn reason I can't stop smiling…

Chapter Eighteen

MICHAEL

As we walk into the kitchen, I'm still wholly shocked that I was able to make Regina laugh. I mean, even with those who I haven't rubbed the wrong way, I'm not considered the funniest. It's nice someone finally gets my humor, though.

Now I have my own smile that just won't go away. I hope it doesn't look too goofy or anything, but I just can't help myself.

"Michael, that really was a good one," Regina says, still chuckling as she leans against the counter. "I mean, a borderline pun, but still. Nice one."

"Thanks," I say, settling next to her. I'm glad we can linger in this moment. It's better than stewing in annoyance or quasi-hatred or something. I wonder if it's something we can keep all night long. And after wondering that, I'm determined to keep this mood, this lightness.

"Gosh, I just need a moment." Regina sighs and rolls her shoulders back a few times. "We needed to be done with that. All of this paperwork and tax statement and stuff is seeming worse and worse with each day. I feel like we won't ever get through it."

"We will. I mean, I've even done worse. Some things just take longer than others. And besides, your mother's bakery had— I mean, it has— so much history, a lot more than most places. It's been through a lot, which means we have to go through a lot."

"When you say it that way, we sound more noble." She turns to me and smiles. I have to say… Regina is beautiful even without smiling, with her normal expression. But when she cracks a grin, her whole face lights up, and I'm dumbstruck. Those big brown eyes, ebony skin that glows. Can she tell I'm looking at her this deeply?

"So, what're we making?" I ask, fumbling for words.

"I don't know. Maybe Chicken and Dumplings?" she asks. "Do you like those?"

"I don't know if I've ever had that kind of dumpling. I mean, I've had it like the ones in the Chinese restaurants. Is it like that?"

"No…" I can see her getting more excited. "Chicken and Dumplings are a Southern dish. You make some chicken, and then you boil the dumplings in the broth. It's warm. My mama always made them from scratch, and we'd eat them every Monday in the wintertime using extra dough from the bakery. It was our thing." Regina begins glowing even brighter. "We *have* to make them."

"Of course," I answer immediately, though I have to admit I'm only going along with her because of this magnetism her words have at this moment. Also, I'm hoping that whatever we make doesn't have too much garlic in it…

"Oh, you poor little Chicago boy. You don't even know how good these are. But you'll see soon enough. What *do* you know how to make?" She turns and begins pulling flour and other dry ingredients, presumably for the dough, out of the cabinets.

"I mean, I can make most things." I catch the white canister of baking powder she throws at me, marveling at the harmony we are displaying. It's as if our brains are connecting on a different wavelength.

Even better, I'm getting gladder by the second at Regina's suggestion to eat here instead of out. This way

I'll get to spend more time with her alone. Whether this combination is a recipe for a disaster or a heartache (or a loving flavor in disguise) I'm not yet sure.

"My mama taught me how to make this years ago when I was younger, and I've been making them ever since," Regina says. There's something to her tone whenever she speaks about her small little town or her mother or her past, I notice. It's softer, more nostalgic.

Most of the time, she seems to have her firm executive persona on. Talking about her family or her home is the only thing to get her out of that mode. I like her better this way. She seems more comfortable, more real.

"I can follow a recipe pretty well, but I'm not like a chef or something. My family didn't do much cooking, but there were always tons of food trucks and restaurants around, so we ate well."

"Yeah… Mama liked to cook for us a few times a week, but she was always so busy with the bakery that we learned to cook for ourselves or eat off leftovers to give her a break sometimes. Bridgid has always been the better baker, but I think I'm better when it comes to the entrees, you know? Her dumplings are always— and don't tell her I told you— a little doughy." Regina says the last part in a whisper, her eyes twinkling.

She sure is something. I mutter to myself as I bend down by the island and pull out a bowl. From there we begin the cooking process. Regina puts on a pot of water with chicken for its first round while I begin making the dough, following the instructions she feeds to me periodically.

We move around the kitchen and each so fluidly. An outsider would probably think we have been making meals together for years, such beautiful chemistry. It feels good, too. The longer I'm doing it, the righter it becomes.

I think this is the first day since I've come that I've felt a happiness this intense. Actually, it may be the first time in my life I've felt this much joy and contentment. Here I am making dinner with a beautiful girl who smiles at me every time I glance over at her. You'd think it was a dream (I have already pinched myself twice to make sure).

Once the dough is ready, we're still waiting on the pot of chicken to boil for a second time, so we lean against the counter parallel to it and wait for a while, our arms crossed. Regina and I both stare for a while, and then we finally turn to each other.

She doesn't look away.

I don't either.

Chapter Nineteen

"So," Michael says.

"Yep."

Our eyes are locked on one another. If I didn't know there was a pot of chicken boiling, I'd think the steam in the kitchen is coming from us. Thank god we set a timer. There's no way I can concentrate on how long the chicken's been going for. It could be thirty seconds or thirty minutes.

In the charged silence between us, there's something else I become keenly aware of. The house is empty.

It's not a surprise. Bridgid is hardly ever here. She's spending all her time with Joel. Katrina seems to come and go seemingly at random, but never lingering for long. I've been worried it's because she doesn't like being around Michael and I arguing all the time. Katrina's always saying how she 'absorbs whatever energy' is around her, and that too many 'negative vibes' impact her health.

In other words, Michael and I are alone. There's little danger of anyone walking in on us. I could have him sit me up on the counter and shove his head between my legs and not worry about –

Whoa, sister. Slow your roll there.

I clear my throat at the same time as I try to clear that image from my mind. "We need to chop up some parsley. Check the fridge."

He pops his head in and finds a bag near the back. I tell him to chop it up fine. He sets to work and after a moment asks, "Like this?"

I lean over his shoulder to check his handiwork. I nearly settle my chin on his shoulder, I'm feeling so comfortable. I have to remind myself this is the first time we're in a kitchen together. We're colleagues, not a couple.

"Looks great," I say, and quickly turn away.

The timer beeps.

"Okay," I announce, back at the stove. "Time to add the dumplings. Ready?"

He has to move past me again to get to the prepped dumplings. Our bodies brush against each other. It's the kind of touch that, if it happened between two strangers, you'd immediately recoil and apologize. Neither of us do that. I feel the tension build even more, and there's an ache beginning to grow at the pit of my stomach.

Michael picks up a handful of dumplings. "Drop 'em in," I tell him.

He starts letting them plop into the pot. They splash and some of the hot soup hits my hand. I wince and shake the hand.

"Geez, easy there, mister…"

"Oh, shit, I'm sorry!"

"It's okay…" I mutter, inspecting my hand.

"Let me see…"

"It's not bad."

He takes my barely singed hand in his. His fingers are more delicate than I imagined. Which makes me imagine all the things he could do with those fingers.

"I don't think we need to amputate," he says.

"Good for you, or you'd starve. Keep adding the dumplings." He grabs another handful. I place my hand on his over the pot. The hot steam envelops our hands.

It's like they could melt into each other. "Go gently this time," I tell him.

Slowly, one by one, he places the dumpling in the pot. When he's done, we separate. But the feel of him lingers near my skin, like he was a bit of flour streaked across my apron.

"How do we know when they're done?"

"The toothpick test," I say, grabbing a shot glass loaded with them.

He reaches out and takes one, slips it into his mouth. "You know," he says, teeth clenched around it, "for about three months in high school I went around every day with one of these in my mouth."

"You didn't."

"Swear to God."

"Did you have some sort of oral fixation?"

"I thought it looked cool." He narrows his eyes like he's James Dean or something, drops his chin. It's ridiculous. I try for a second not to just laugh outright at him. But he keeps it up, mugging, raising his eyebrows one at a time, furrowing his brow, and I can't help it. First, it's just air blowing through my lips, then I double over with a belly laugh.

"You thought that looked cool?"

He shrugs, takes the toothpick out of his mouth. "I think I saw it in a movie or something."

"If Mama saw you walking around with that thing hanging off your lips, she'd smack it right out."

"I could have used Mama, in that case."

"She knew how to steer everybody straight. I know you can't tell from the mess of paperwork she left behind —"

"No," he interrupts, "I can tell. From her daughters."

There's that charged silence again. The house is empty, I remember again, and it's like there's no one else in the world except him and me.

And our stomachs. There's another growl and he puts his hand on his belly and grimaces. "I think that was mine, this time. Can we test the dumplings?" He makes like he's going to stick the toothpick he just had in his mouth into the soup.

"Ew! Not with that dirty thing." I playfully hip check him out of the way. His hand accidentally brushes my rear as he backs off. It sends a wave of heat up my spine and across my back. I sweat a little and not from the steaming pot below me.

"Done," I say, removing a clean toothpick from a dumpling. "Toss in the parsley and let's eat."

A few minutes later, the bowls are full and steaming as we set ourselves down at the kitchen table. We've gone faux fancy: placemats, cloth napkins, spoons *and* forks. We stopped short of lighting candles. Probably for the better. Good lord, if we set that sort of romantic mood, I'm not sure I'd get very far into the meal…

"Mmmm," he says, taking a big spoonful. Then, he opens his mouth wide and breathes in and out hurriedly. "Hot! Hot!" he cries, mouth full.

"You dummy, blow on it first," I say.

He swallows with a groan.

I demonstrate blowing on the soup. And, yeah, I make it a little more dirty than necessary. Then I slowly take the spoon into my mouth.

He watches my lips carefully. "It came out really delicious," he says.

I swallow. "Yeah. It's not half-bad actually."

He's looking down at his soup, so he doesn't notice the way my eyes are locked on him as I say that.

Chapter Twenty

MICHAEL

I must be hungrier than I realize, because I devour the first bowl of chicken and dumplings. It really is good. Not that there is any one particular thing that makes it stand out in some special way. There's no 'secret ingredient' that makes my mind explode. It's more that I can literally taste the homemade-ness of it. It tastes of this house. Of this family.

Maybe it's stretching things too far, but… it even tastes a little bit of Regina, as well. As though I'm somehow learning about her just from eating a meal she's made. You probably think that sounds stupid and I don't care. It's how I feel.

I'm scraping the bottom of my bowl before she's even half-way through hers. I hop up to grab myself another ladle full. So that I don't come across as an incredible pig, I repeat, "This is so tasty, I swear to god, I can't get enough."

"If I didn't know better," she responds from the table, "I'd think you were trying to butter me up."

I watch the dumplings slide into the soup in my bowl. They are so firm and lush that I can't help but think of Regina's breasts as I stare at them. So maybe I'm a little distracted when I announce, "Seriously, I could eat like this for the rest of my life."

Turning back to the table with my bowl, I suddenly hear what I just said. If *I* didn't know better, that sounded like a borderline marriage proposal! What is going on with me? I try to gauge how Regina heard the words as I sit back down.

She's staring at me. There's a hunger in her eyes that I realize has nothing to do with the hunger in her belly. Maybe with a hunger a little further south…? Thinking of that sends a rush of blood south in my own body. My cock swells and starts to get erect, pushing at my thigh and my pants. Thank god I'm already seated.

"Well," she says finally, which even though it breaks the tension of the moment does nothing to relieve my hard-on, "too bad you'll be back in Chicago while I'm still down here."

I shift, trying to get comfortable and to give my engorged member some wiggle room. I dip my spoon into the bowl and say, "Guess I'll have to have some of this shipped up to me."

"Think you can afford the handling fees?" she asks, playfully.

If I didn't know better, I'd think it was *sexually* playful. My imagination certainly reacts like that's how she meant it. At the mention of 'handling' I'm thinking about her hands on my erection, my hands on her ass…

In my distraction, I swallow a barely chewed dumpling and nearly choke. I cough a few times. Thankfully, it breaks the spell, because resisting her is becoming more and more difficult.

I know we talk as I finish the rest of my second helping, but I have no idea what we're talking about. My mind is somewhere else. Stuck between fantasies of fucking her on various kitchen surfaces and reminders that my life is back in Chicago, not here – not with her.

Eventually, there's a lull in the conversation. It's not a drop in energy, though. There's a kind of *anticipation* hanging over us in the silence. No doubt about it, she's still looking at me with that hunger. The situation has the unmistakable feel of a 'shit or get off the pot' moment. Or maybe it's a 'kiss or forever stay apart' moment.

Despite every nerve ending in my body loudly voicing its opinion of what to do, my brain tells me to go with what's behind door number two.

"I think I'm all done," I say, rising and officially cutting the metaphysical sexual cord stretched taut between us. She reaches for my bowl, but I keep heading for the sink. "No, no, you relax. I'm responsible for the dishes, right?"

She melts into her chair, lounging and throwing an arm over the back of the chair. The posture thrusts her chest up and out. It takes all my will to maintain eye contact and not look at her gorgeous breasts. I'm not one hundred percent certain that I'm successful.

I hurriedly grab her bowl and bring it to the sink, as well. I get the hot water going and scrub furiously with a sponge, trying to relieve my sexual frustration on the dishes, pots, and pans.

Fortunately, with my body turned to the sink, there's no chance of her catching sight of my hard-on.

As I'm doing the dishes, I hear Regina say, "Man, white boys really *don't* have asses, do they?"

She's checking me out? Really? That's great. But also, hey, that was kind of insulting. "Please don't stare at my ass," I say with mock offense.

"What do you mean? There's no ass to stare at," she retorts.

I give her a little shake.

She whoops.

We both laugh.

It takes every ounce of willpower I have to not spin around and grab her up in my arms and shove my tongue into her mouth. Not to mention the other places I'd put my tongue.

As I work, she gets up and starts handing things to me to wash. She brings everything to me one at time. Which I know doesn't seem odd, but it would be really easy, for example, to just bring over the cutting board with the dirty knives and measuring spoons all together, rather than piecemeal. Is it possible she's using it as excuses to get close to me?

My plan is just to wash the dishes and leave everything on the drying rack. However, between her body constantly coming near me and her breath lingering on my neck every time she leans in to drop something in the sink, my dick refuses to stand down.

I end up drying every dish and then putting everything away before my member stands down.

With a deep breath, I turn back to Regina to say my goodnights. The minute my eyes land back on her, though, I feel the blood rushing south yet again.

Chapter Twenty-One

Dinner's done. Dishes are done. But I don't want him to leave. There's an anticipation building up in me. It's gripping my bones and telling me to keep this night going.

"Hey," I say as he's drying his hands at the sink, "what about a drink before you go back to the hotel?"

He seems to hesitate a moment. Crap. Should I not have done that? No… there's something else in that hesitation, I think. Maybe he's feeling the same pull I am – in both directions, just like me?

"Sure," he says, sliding the towel back on the rack. "That'd be great."

We make our way to the family room. The old house is still full of a life from knickknack collecting on Mama's part, and the family room is the hub. While I pour the drinks, I keep an eye on Michael as he explores the various bits of folk crafts scattered around. He finally stops at the collection of porcelain dogs on the mantle.

"These are cute," Michael says of the dogs as I hand him the drink. I've poured us some bourbon. It's possible the drinks are fairly taller than average.

"Mama got obsessed with them for a while right after we all moved out. It made Christmas and birthday shopping for her easy. But I never understood it."

"I had an aunt who collected porcelain dogs. Not just dogs, either. Like, porcelain Disney characters, porcelain penguins, porcelain thirties movie characters… she had an entire Marx Brothers set. It was so weird. This is much more restrained."

"Mama would be glad to know that. Cheers."

We clink glasses. I notice he takes a long sip of his drink. I do, too. The warm flush of the alcohol seems to embolden everything I'm feeling. The consequence is that my mind is at a loss for words. I'm afraid if I open my mouth now, the only thing that's going to come out is, "Fuck me."

Fortunately, he breaks the silence and says, "It's hard for me to imagine you growing up in this house."

"Oh? Why is that?"

"It's so…"

"Careful," I warn, playfully. "Don't ruin the nice evening we're having."

"It's just that this place feels very far from the kind of gung-ho corporate world you wound up in."

"Hm. I can't tell if me or the house should be complimented, insulted, or both."

"Just an observation. I guess I'm trying to picture little Regina running around here."

I laugh into my glass. "Oh, and I can just imagine what little Michael was like."

He takes another deep drink and leans against the mantle. "I've gotta hear this."

"Okay. Um…" I glance up and down his body pretending to try and picture him in teenage form, and not picturing him grown-up and naked. "Let's see. Class President. Not the kind who ran on a 'better school lunches' platform. You were one of those Class Presidents who had some grandiose ideas like getting the principal to recognize the Rwanda genocide or Earth Day or something."

His turn to laugh. Something about the way he does makes my hips want to sway in rhythm.

"I wish I could say that was accurate. Truth is, I was pretty aimless in school," he says.

"Oh, too cool for it, I guess?"

"Bored, mostly."

"Class clown, then?"

"Nope. I was like the class mastermind."

"I've never heard of that. Explain."

"For example," he starts, "my senior year, my class pulled off an impressive prank on the vice principal. He drove one of the new VW bugs – ya know, with the little flower on the dashboard? The last day of the semester before Christmas break, we got that thing up on the roof of the school. The final bell rang, and everyone ran out to watch him go look for his car."

I laugh, picturing it as he laughs remembering it. "Now," he continues between laughs, "I was not involved in the actual carrying out of the prank… But *I* told the people who were how to do it."

"You little scoundrel."

"When the vice principal found out, he wasn't sure whether to suspend me or graduate me early."

We laugh again. I try to remember the last time I felt this free, this fun. My instinct is to say, 'not since Donovan'.

But the truth is — I think it goes back even further than that.

Meanwhile, the alcohol is making quick work through my veins. On top of that, his voice, his looks, his laugh are all making quick work through other parts of me. I can feel myself loosening. Preparing to let go. I *want* to let go. It would feel so good…

"So," I say, wagging a finger at him and leaning in like we're sharing something confidential, "I can see I have to keep my eye on you."

He leans in, too. "Is that so bad?" he asks, his voice low. It seems to vibrate on the same frequency as my body.

"Hm," I say and take a sip of my drink.

Just like I'd hoped, that 'hm' intrigues him and leans in even more. "What's that mean?"

"Just that we'll have to see."

We're so close now. He's looking at me like he's just crossed the Sahara and I am a deep, inviting well.

Which I may as well be. I can feel myself getting wet. I could take him inside me so easily, so quickly. To get it started, I would barely even have to reach out, that's how close we are. A slight inclination forward of my head and our lips would be locked and from there it would be a short hop, skip and jump to getting the satisfaction my body is craving.

But something holds me back. I don't jump his bones. I don't move closer for a kiss. I take a sip of my drink. I turn away from him and point out some other little crafty collection of Mama's.

The moment passes. The desire does not.

Chapter Twenty-Two

MICHAEL

I can't believe I'm telling her the stupid senior prank story. I haven't told that story in years. It's a relief to see that she seems to be enjoying it.

I'm impressed I can even make my way through the story without my words devolving into nonsense syllables. Everything about her is distracting. Her smile, the glow in her eyes as I relay my teenage hijinks, all of it makes me feel discombobulated.

It's like I'm already drunk from her, and the bourbon is just making me even loopier. As I tell the story about my senior year, I start to *feel* like a teenager again: a glorious mess of horndog and goofball.

She laughs at the story. Her breath is warm. I imagine that it is alive with electricity. As it brushes against my skin, it's like it sends little shockwaves straight through me to my groin. I can hear a rushing between my ears as the blood pumps harder and harder through my body.

My erection is back. (*It's alive!* I think) One glance down and she'd be able to see how badly I want her.

She takes another sip of her drink and it leaves a little drop of bourbon on her lower lip. That lip looks delicious. Full, pink and warm. Her tongue slides out and licks the drop away. I can imagine that tongue sliding along the shaft of my prick, I can imagine it filling my mouth…

I try to figure out how to play this.

I could just sweep her up in my arms, damn the torpedoes and all that. Just put my mouth on hers and trust that what I think is going on between us is really going on.

Then there's the mature thing, which would be to mention my feelings. The problem with words, though, is that you can't take them back. Sure, you can talk and then decide *not* to take action. But the words are still out there. Whereas, if I do nothing, well, there's nothing that needs to be discussed.

I certainly don't want to pressure her. I'm not even one hundred percent certain I should be pursuing her. Maybe this is all just a consequence of the pressure cooker of that little office where we've been working on her mother's finances. Throw two hard-nosed people together like that, there's bound to be sparks. That doesn't mean you need to start a fire.

Then I tell myself to stop overthinking this. We had a pleasant dinner. We're enjoying a drink. The attraction between us is palpable. There's only one way this goes, you know it, she knows it, so just let the inevitable happen --

But then something shifts.

It's barely noticeable at first. Just a hint that something just got switched off. She's pulling away. Turning from me to show me something on a side table – some Native American crafts her mom was fond off.

Did I do something wrong? For a moment, I stare at the empty space where she was just standing a second ago, looking for all the world like she wanted me. A small panic begins to assert itself. Did I cross a line? Was my hard-on obvious and insulting?

No. Calm down, moron.

It's obvious what just happened. She's got the same doubts that I've got. Only she's smarter than I am. She put a stop to where things were going.

The rush of my pounding blood dissipates. I can hear normally again. My erection retreats, embarrassed, like someone who just walked into the wrong bathroom. My balls feel like they weigh a ton and I regret not being able to give them any quick resolution.

It's the right decision, I think, to not let this go any further. Doesn't make it feel any better. I literally have to suppress a groan of disappointment.

I feign interest in the things Regina is talking about. The conversation goes on for another four or five minutes, but the flow is all wrong, now. We're talking over each other. It becomes halting, full of awkward stops and starts.

Finally, I throw the rest of my drink back.

"You want another?" she asks, starting to rise from the couch where she's stationed herself.

"No, no," I say quickly, "I should, uh, I should get back to the hotel."

She slowly lowers herself back onto the couch. "Mm. Mm-hm. Right."

There's an awkward pause. Both of us looking for some reason to extend the night. Both of us wondering if my going away is the right decision or not.

"So… thanks for that dinner. It was amazing."

"It was all right."

"A little better than all right."

"…okay."

Another weird lull. For two people who passed the time so easily, these last two minutes are taking an eternity to get through.

I should just say goodnight. Instead, I prolong the agony. "So, I guess tomorrow we'll dive back in."

"Yup. Dive *right* on in."

"Right." Another pause. Jesus, this is terrible. "I think we're close to done, actually."

"We ought to be, right?"

"Yep."

Pause. Awkwardly. I'm sweating like I'm about to deliver a speech I'm not prepared for or something. This is horrible.

"Well. G'night!" I say, much too loudly.

"I'll show you to the door," she says, rising.

"Oh."

That throws a wrinkle in things. I didn't anticipate her walking me to the door. That's the sort of thing that can end in a kiss, right? Like, a goodnight kiss.

We get to the door. She drops her hand on the knob. It lingers there. "Well…" she says with a dramatic exhale.

"Yeah."

If I kissed her, I don't think she'd make me stop. If I kissed her, I think we'd be naked and in bed in moments. If I kissed her, I don't think I'd ever want to stop kissing her.

So of course I say, "See you tomorrow morning."

She nods. She opens the door. I step outside.

"Not *too* early," she calls out jokingly.

Before I can turn back and offer some joke in return, she's closed the door and I'm alone in the night with my unfulfilled desires.

Chapter Twenty-Three

I close the front door before he can say anything else. Before either of us has another chance to make a mistake. Because that's what it would be, right? A mistake?

Once he's gone, for what seems like the first time in hours, I can exhale fully. "Whoo," I announce to the empty house, leaning back against the front door. I put a palm to my forehead. I'm warm and flush. I try to pretend it's just from the alcohol.

I stay at the door until I can hear Michael's rental car start up and pull away. There's a palpable disappointment that runs through my mid-section. I remind myself that a little disappointment now is better than a lot of regret later. That seems to work.

Turning off the lights downstairs, I try to not to notice that the house still smells like him. I make my way upstairs and force myself to take a nice, warm shower. I let the warm water wash away the desire I've been feeling in my arms, my breasts, my pussy. After the shower, I pat my body dry, put on some fresh panties and a t-shirt, and hop into bed.

I'm hoping the warm shower and the alcohol will combine to put me right to sleep. I am *not* that lucky.

Instead, I spend the next few hours tossing and turning. My head is a mess of different thoughts and emotions. All of them about Michael, of course. I try to remind myself how angry he makes me. Which only reminds me of how that kind of turns me on. Then I think about how he made me laugh. Which is when I have to remind myself that he is leaving for Chicago as soon as the work on Mama's finances is done.

Gather ye rosebuds while ye may, one side of me tells the other.

Don't stick your hands in an open flame, the other side of me tells the first one.

Back and forth like that. The clock reads three in the morning and I groan into my pillows. After trying every single position I can think of or that I've ever fallen asleep in, my body is still alive and very much craving Michael.

I'm on my side with a pillow between my knees. I hug the pillow in tight. I keep my eyes closed. It's just a test, I tell myself. Maybe if I give my body just a little attention, it'll relax, and I'll fall asleep.

It doesn't work. My body longs for the pillow to be Michael's body between my legs. I pull it in closer and, without meaning to, I start gently humping it, like some teenage girl.

I guess this is happening. I have a moment of regret that I never listened to a friend of mine who swore no woman should travel anywhere without a dildo. Guess we're going old school.

I let myself roll fully onto my back and discard the pillow. I slide my hands up under my t-shirt and handle my breasts, softly, like I can imagine Michael doing. As I think about his lips on my nipples, I give them a little squeeze.

Still rubbing at my breasts with one hand, I slip a hand down between my legs. My panties are wet. I gently work on myself through the fabric.

I let myself build up slowly. Little jolts of joy shoot out from my center and down to my heels. I give a few tiny gasps as my body thanks me for finally giving it what it's wanted all night.

Well. Not completely. Michael's not here. But I can imagine. I can imagine the heaviness of him on top of me as we kiss. I can imagine how his ass will feel in my hands as I open my legs wide for him.

My lips purse in pretend kisses as I slide my damp panties off. I imagine how his mouth might feel, warm and full, on my pussy. In the real world, my hand rubs all along myself, then my fingers play with my clit.

Trying to anticipate how his tongue might be on me, I work it in a combination of quick little circles, then slow massages. The desire builds. I put my fingers in my mouth to wet them and then slide two fingers slowly inside myself.

"Ohh, Michael…" I mutter, losing myself in the fantasy.

I can almost feel his breath, hot and strong, against my neck. My need vocalizes itself in little moans.

I go in and out quickly, imagining its Michael's cock long and hard sliding inside me. My lips press together as I give higher and higher exclamations of joy. With my free hand, I pull my t-shirt up and over my breasts and begin to massage them with the same rapid rhythm I'm fucking myself with.

There's lightning going off in every muscle of my body. I trust in the house still being empty and quiet and let my moans grow in volume.

Then I've got both hands between my legs. One going crazy on my clit while the other slides in and out. My legs butterfly up and down as I get closer and closer, the ache I've had all night finally having its needs met.

I cum harder than I have in a long time. Wave upon wave of ecstasy crackling through me. I keep playing with myself even as I continue to cum and I imagine Michael's throbbing member deep inside me still. I call out his name, "Michael, yes, yes!" My legs shake.

At last, I go limp. I gently caress my tender breasts. I slowly massage my clit, letting it have the last of its fill.

Finally, I'm exhausted. My body is completely satisfied, and it lets my brain know that we can go to sleep.

I pull the covers back over my naked body. Dammit, I feel good.

I fall asleep with Michael's name on my lips.

Chapter Twenty-Four

MICHAEL

Somehow, I stay hard the entire car ride back to my hotel. All I can think about is all the things that could've happened tonight. I remind myself that there is a reason neither of us took it there... a very good and sane reason. But my mind always goes back to the what-ifs.

It's different when you're sexually attracted to someone for more than what you see what you look at them on the outside. What turns me on so much about Regina is not her physical appearance. That's not to say her appearance doesn't turn me on- I'd be lying if I said it didn't. But that's not the thing that makes me rock hard whenever I'm near her.

It's her aura, her strong personality. Her confidence… her sureness. Her energy. Hell, even her infuriating attitude is sexy. She's a magnificent woman, and I knew it the moment we met. I knew I was in trouble, instantly.

And that's why I keep convincing myself that I can't go there with her. If I go there, I can never go back. If I go there, I ruin the image of her in my head and I get the real thing. And the real thing is so much more precious than what I dream up in my head. The real thing is delicate. I can't risk ruining that. She is too great of a person. I just can't risk something going wrong between us.

Besides, I'm not here permanently. That's something that's been weighing in my mind since I got here. I tell myself every night that I can't get too attached to anything here- especially not Regina. Because in the end, I'll be boarding a flight to Chicago with my one-way ticket.

Despite all of that, my mind still drifts to what Regina's naked skin against mine would feel like. I park my car and realize that I don't even know how I drove to the hotel in one piece, I was deep in my fantasies the entire ride.

As soon as I get in, I strip off my clothes and throw them into a pile at the end of my bed. I decide to have a cold shower to hopefully wash away these thoughts about Regina, so I can actually get some sleep tonight.

I soap myself up, letting the shower water hit my back in just the right spot. I start to imagine Regina's hands making their way up and down my back. I bet she gives a good massage. My mind wanders to an image of her digging her nails into my back as she screams in ecstasy. I can already feel my hard-on springing back up.

Welp, that only lasted about five minutes.

Turning around, I turn the hot water all the way up, and finally decide to take matters into my own hands, literally, and do something about all these fantasies. Maybe if I give my body a little bit of a release, it can calm the fuck down for a minute or two.

I begin to slowly massage my cock, starting at the tip and working my way all the way down. I close my eyes and let the shower steam envelope me, while I imagine that it's Regina's hands on me instead of my own.

In my mind, Regina gently grasps my balls in one hand, and slowly begins massaging them while she speeds up the other hand that's sliding up and down my shaft. I imagine her bringing her mouth down and sucking on my balls before sliding her tongue up along my shaft until she reaches the tip. She winks and smiles up at me, a mix of angelic and devilish, before plunging my cock all the way to the back of her throat.

I imagine her stopping just when I'm about to bust, a little payback for all the times I've pissed her off. But she wants me just as bad I want her, so she stands up and turns around, so her cheek is pressed against the wall. She puts both hands at the small of her back, as if she were bound, and sticks her ass out towards me.

Even in my imagination she's sexier than ever. I grab her ass with both hands, squeezing. I've dreamed of getting my hands on this thing since the moment I dared to look at it. Giving it a little smack, I take her wrists in one hand to secure them, while I massage my cock against her clit, making her long for it a little more.

I tease her entrance, making like I'm about to put it in and then quickly pulling away. I can practically hear her groaning and begging me to just give it to her already.

Finally, I imagine myself doing the thing I know we've both been craving since we locked eyes. I slowly push my long, thick cock into her, until my balls slap against her clit. I can hear her breath hitching, shocked at my length and how good it feels inside her.

I give her a few thrusts to get used to it, and then I go wild. I fuck her while she begs me not to stop. I have to slap her ass just to stop myself from coming, which seems to drive her even crazier.

I let her wrists go, and she immediately clings to the wall with her hands for dear life. I bring my now free hand up to her neck and wrap my fingers around it ever so slightly.

"Tighter," she gasps.

Tightening my grip, I decide neither of us can wait any longer. I pound her with everything I have, causing Regina to emit sounds I've never heard before. She comes just seconds before I do, but her orgasm drives me so wild that I can't help but come with her.

Back to reality, I'm practically shaking from the pleasure I just felt. I've never come so hard in my life… if just fantasizing about her does *this* to me… I can't even *imagine* what she would actually feel like.

I wash myself off and finish up my shower. I'm in such a daze I don't even remember walking out of the bathroom, but I throw myself into bed, butt naked and let myself doze off, not even bothering with the sheets. I dream of her all night.

Chapter Twenty-Five

REGINA

When I wake up in the morning, I feel surprisingly rested for the first time in forever. Maybe it's because I finally gave my body a sliver of what it's been wanting for weeks now. Either way, I'm ready to start the day.

That is, until I realize that I'm going to have to look Michael in the eye knowing what I did last night. Fuck, I didn't think about that. I feel like a teenage girl all over again, nervous to face her crush.

Shaking my head, I decide to use this to my advantage. Every time Michael pisses me off, I'm going to think about how much pleasure I felt last night imagining that it was him touching me. I'll even imagine sitting on his face to shut him up if I have to.

I choose a black top that's mostly sheer and throw on some leggings to really show off my ass. I'm usually dressed very professionally, like I would if I were going into work- but not today. Today I'm going to tease him a little, I want him to look at me and be unable to focus.

The truth is- I was so ready to give myself to him last night. I did everything I could to show him that I was open- even invited him to stay for drinks for god's sake. If he had kissed me, I wouldn't have stopped him. But he didn't, and I'm going to make him pay for that today.

I don't even bother with makeup other than some mascara and some sheer gloss. I know it won't be my face that he's going to be staring at. A few minutes before he arrives, I put some tea on, making a little extra in case he wants some.

As soon as I hear the knock at the door, my heart races. I feel a little thrill in my stomach and will myself to calm down before heading to the door. Taking a deep breath, I let him in. I avoid eye contact, but I can feel his eyes glazing over my body. I lead him to the kitchen, purposely swaying my ass.

"You want some tea? I just put some on."

"Yeah- yeah uh, sure I'll take some."

There's something different in the way he's talking to me, but I can't quite put my finger on it.

"It should be done in a few minutes," I say, leaning against the counter and crossing my arms under my breasts, making them pop out even more.

I watch him carefully, seeing how he carefully avoids looking at my face. I can tell he's trying not to look, but eventually his eyes win, and he glances at my breasts. Men are so obvious; he's practically drooling over there. I decide to take it a step further, bending down to grab some mugs out of the dishwasher, my ass in his direction.

Turning around, I see that his face is beet red. I almost feel bad for him… almost. The tea seems to be taking longer than I thought, and we stand there in awkward silence for a bit.

"Actually I think I'm gonna head into the office and get everything started, would you bring me my tea in there?" he asks.

Not even waiting for a response, he scurries down the hall. Maybe I'm being a bit too mean. Once the tea is done, I bring our mugs into the office.

"Thank you," he says, making eye contact for the first time since he arrived.

Now it's my turn to blush. We lock eyes and I immediately think of how I touched myself to the thought of him last night.

"You're welcome," I say, quickly turning away so he doesn't notice anything.

We work in silence for a good hour or so, almost in harmony. We seem to be getting things done, no one is offending anyone, no one is giving the silent treatment. And then the bastard has to go and ruin it.

"Can you handle this one? The entire thing is completely illegible," he says, handing me a packet of papers.

That insipid fuck. How can one person be so callous? Doesn't he realize that every time he says something like this, he's insulting my dead mother?

I rip the paper out of his hands, slamming it down on my end of the desk. I can't take this anymore. Standing up so aggressively that my chair falls over, I turn to him.

He stands up too, ready to go, but still with a twinge of fear in his eyes. We stare for a moment, the silence deafening. Then we roar.

"Why do you take offense to *every* fucking thing I say?! All I'm trying to do is the job I was hired for!" he screams.

"Yeah? Do you speak to everyone that hires you this way?? Mama would be ashamed to have someone like you in her house."

Considering how highly we all speak of Mama; I know that one stings him. And I don't care one bit.

"I'm done. I can't do this anymore," Michael says, an animalistic look on his face.

"Good!!" I shout, turning to leave.

"No," he says, grabbing my wrist and pulling me back. "I *mean*, I can't do *this* anymore."

He looks me right in the eye, his grip on my wrist tightening. Before I have a chance to respond, he pulls my body up against his, and plants his lips on mine at the same time.

Shocked, I immediately pull away, my eyes questioning his. But all I find there is desire- pure desire. I surrender myself to him, allowing him to kiss me this time, allowing myself to feel it. And it feels better than any fantasy I could've dreamed up.

Our lips collide and I breathe him in, savoring it. A moan slips out of both of us as we dual in a different way than we have been since he arrived. I grab a handful of his hair, pulling him even closer, as he does the same, hand on the back of my neck pressing me into him.

Michael's lips on mine feels like two pieces of a puzzle connecting, as cheesy as that may sound. I now know why I've been so drawn to him… because this right here feels so right.

Chapter Twenty-Six

MICHAEL

I couldn't help it, I had to have her. That little comment about her mother drove me right over the edge. The nerve this woman has, it's just so powerful. I couldn't let her walk out of this room without kissing her. And I will never regret it… this feels so amazing.

I've had good first kisses before, but nothing like this. This is easily the best kiss I have had and will ever have. Regina tastes so good on my lips; it just feels so perfectly right. We're so in sync, much like we were while cooking together last night.

I've never felt so pulled to one person like the pull I've felt to Regina, and now I know exactly why. It's like we're magnetized to each other. I need more of her, now.

I begin trailing my lips down her neck, along her collar bone, up the other side of her neck, and finally land on her ear. I nibble at it, loving the way it makes her hairs stand up. She lets out little gasps as I gently kiss and nibble at her.

Suddenly she can't take it anymore, pulling me back to her lips. I push her into the wall, putting my hand around her neck just like I did in my little fantasy of her last night. She loves it, just as I imagined she would. The more we kiss, the more I tighten my hand around her neck. She's smiling while she gasps for more breath. Damn this girl is sexy.

Her hands trail down my body, ripping my shirt off and exploring my chest. She trails her lips down further and further, past my belly button. She stops just at the button on my jeans, smiles, and trails kisses all the way back up to my chest.

We kiss as she explores the muscles on my back, until she reaches my ass and grabs a hold, pushing me into her. My hard cock is pressed into her stomach now, and the moment she feels it she lets out a little gasp, as if in surprise.

Feeling myself pressed into her, after all those times of trying to hide how hard I was, after how hard I came last night just thinking of her… I can't handle this. I pull off her black sheer top that I know she wore just to bother me and kiss every inch of her in sight.

It took everything in me not to rip that black lace bra off the moment I saw it, but I can't wait any longer. I rip it off, hearing the lace tearing and not giving one fuck. I grab one full breast into my hand, squeezing it hard. She winces, but immediately follows it with a naughty smile.

"Don't worry about being gentle with me," she whispers. And how could I disobey her?

I pick her up and move her so that she's sitting atop the desk.

I start off by trailing kisses all over her breast, avoiding the nipple. Just when she looks like she's about to shove it in my mouth herself, I very gently kiss her nipple. Teasing it with my tongue, I use my other hand to play with the opposite one.

Finally, I go in. I graze my teeth against her nipple a few times, before taking it in my mouth and biting down, running my teeth back and forth over it. I can hear her whimpering as I bite harder, squeezing her nipple in between my teeth and moving it around in a circular motion, occasionally adding my tongue to the mix. But she doesn't pull away, in fact she grabs my head and forces it even closer, as if to tell me not to stop.

She reaches down for my cock, but I shove her hand away. This is about *her* right now. She deserves to feel pleasure, and I can't be distracted while I make that happen.

Once I'm done with one, I move to the other, leaving her very raw nipple stinging in the open air. I replace my mouth with my hand, rubbing it in between my index finger and my thumb. She lets out a small shriek when I touch it, followed by a long moan.

I notice her opening her legs up wide, not even meaning to, as I start in on her free nipple with my teeth. This time she seems to be in even more pain, as I nibble down while rubbing the other one. She trails her hands down her body and into her leggings, beginning to massage her clit. I can see that she's completely lost in another world right now, one mixed with pain and pure pleasure.

She's practically screaming when I pull away. I look into her eyes as I go back to her completely raw nipples. I take one into my mouth, sucking on it and pulling it as far away from her body as I can with my teeth. I can see her struggling internally trying to decide whether it hurts or feels amazing. She loses that battle and surrenders to me, beginning to finger herself.

We keep eye contact as I continue this routine of sucking and pulling at her sore and tender nipples while she fucks herself. I reach down and push my fingers inside of her alongside her own. We both speed up our pace, working at her pussy in unison. I know it's about to happen when she opens her mouth and arches her back, and finally she screams out as she comes.

We pull our fingers out of her at the same time. I take her two fingers into my mouth, sucking them clean, as well as my own, before pulling her to me and kissing her. Her lips cling to me, unwilling to leave mine after the pleasure I just gifted her.

"You aren't even inside of me yet and you're already amazing," she laughs as she still struggles to catch her breath from her orgasm.

We laugh together, before pulling back in for a kiss.

Chapter Twenty-Seven

REGINA

Michael's mouth on my breasts feels so amazing I almost can't handle it. He gives me exactly what I need from him, the perfect mixture of pain and pleasure. The way he bites at my nipples while rubbing the opposite one between his fingers drives me so crazy, I wouldn't even know how to describe the feeling if I was asked to.

The pain I feel while he rubs my raw nipples in between his teeth is exquisite; and the louder I moan, the tighter I grip him- the harder he bites down. The way his eyes never leave mine, like he wants to watch the pleasure roll over me- is so unbelievably sexy.

I try to reach for his cock, I want to make him feel good too, but he shoves my hand away and bites even harder.

It's so nice to be with a man who actually wants to focus on *you*. So much so that he doesn't even want me to touch him while he's pleasuring me.

This man knows *exactly* what he's doing, and no fantasy could ever match up to the real thing. I can't help but touch myself while he tortures my nipples, massaging my clit and then slipping two fingers inside of myself.

Eventually he joins me, driving two of his thick fingers into me alongside mine until I reach completion. This orgasm is even better than the one I gave myself last night. In fact, it's better than any orgasm I've ever had if I'm being brutally honest… and to think he hasn't even entered me yet.

I shiver at the thought of what my orgasm will be like when he fucks me. I already know that whatever is about to happen, is going to make me explode. I can feel how long and thick his cock is and it takes everything in me not to just rip his jeans off and fuck him right here on this desk already.

I could just push him down, straddle him and ride his dick right here. Not like I haven't dreamed of doing just that during every single day we've spent in this office together.

Even though I just came, I want more of him already. I want all of him. My legs are practically shaking, and I almost fall off of my position on the desk before he catches me. We giggle, and he pulls me into another embrace, kissing me full on, like we're the only man and woman in the entire world. And right now in this moment, our lips interlocked… we are.

When the kiss ends, he scoops me into his arms, and I wrap my legs around his waist, squeezing them as hard as I can, pushing myself closer to him. I can feel his member pushing against me, practically teasing me.

I never could have imagined that Michael was packing like this, ever. It all makes sense now though, his cockiness, his sureness, his confidence, all of it. No man has that kind of energy if he ain't packin.

He begins to walk us out of the office, mouth trailing along my neck. Briefly taking his mouth off of my skin, he looks into my eyes.

"Which way to-"

He doesn't even need to finish as I point down the hall to my bedroom. He turns in that direction, squeezing my ass with both hands as we walk, his nails digging in. I've never had a man handle me quite like Michael does. It's almost like he's reading my mind, he knows exactly where to touch me and for how long. He just knows me, and I've never been with a man that knew exactly what my body needed. It's so fucking satisfying.

He carries me into my room, slams the door shut with his foot, and throws me down on the bed. I whimper, but it's not because I don't like the roughness. I crave it. I need it so bad.

Michael leans down, kissing my lips and then trailing kisses all the way down until he reaches my pussy. He gently kisses it over my leggings, making me shiver, before ripping them off along with my thong at the same time.

He drinks me in, seeing every inch of my body all at once. The way he looks at me is so unbelievable, like he's never seen anything so beautiful in all his life. It makes me feel completely comfortable in my nakedness. He looks at me with such desire and hungry need, and I've never felt more beautiful in my entire life than I do in this moment.

Chapter Twenty-Eight

MICHAEL

As Regina lays down before me, I feel like I can't breathe for a moment. Her body, her beauty…is nearly overwhelming. There are moments in your life when you cannot believe that you are lucky enough to be where you are. You think *'how the hell did I deserve this?'*

This is one of those moments.

It's like she's her own planet and her gravity is pulling me in. I can't fight it even if I wanted to. I'm going to crash. Hard. And I'm ready.

"You ok?" she says to me, with a purr in her voice.

I nod.

"I'm better right now than maybe I've ever been," I respond.

Regina smiles at me and it's like the warm glow of the sun.

"Well then," she says, sliding her bare legs against each other, "why don't you come over here and show how good you are?"

She opened her legs to me then, her delicate hands caressing the smooth skin of her thighs while she does.

I slide down to my knees before her, as if in worship. Which, I suppose, I am.

Taking her left calf in my hands, I bring it to my mouth, kissing it tenderly.

Regina shivers under my touch and I keep kissing her leg, gliding up to her knee, her thigh, up to the mound of her womanhood.

She's already wet, glistening, waiting, and wanting for my attentions. I feel her hands cup my head, pulling me into her closer.

"Yes, baby," she whispers in a husky tone, "that's right. That's what I need. Please. Please. Please."

Gripping my hair, she gives me a slight tug towards her, and I don't need any more encouragement.

I slide my own hands under her taut, round ass, holding it firmly, and finally bring my mouth to her.

She shudders and sighs as my tongue makes contact with her wetness.

"Ohhh god, yes," she moans breathily.

I start working her up and down with my mouth, lapping her in like I was a man dying of thirst. She tastes like sweet honey and wine and I couldn't get enough of it.

Almost immediately, Regina starts grinding her hips, pushing herself against me as we found our natural rhythm together.

I tease her clit with my mouth and my tongue, flicking it lightly.

"Damn," she moans. "Fuck don't stop. That's it, Michael, that's it," she mumbles to herself.

I hold firmly onto her as her hips start bucking up and down, using me to find what she needs.

I switch my grip from her ass to the inside of her thighs, pressing them down and spreading them even wider, giving myself even more access to her.

"This is…oh god…this is *so* fucking good," Regina pants. She holds my head firmly and presses herself against my mouth.

I pick my head up for just a moment and look into her eyes.

"Don't hold it," I say, "let it go. Let it crash over you. I want it."

Then I bury myself between her legs again, quickly returning to work.

Regina pulls on my hair so hard that it hurts. (What's more is, I like it.)

"Michael," she says, heat dripping from her tongue, "I'm going to cum. Don't stop. Fuck, don't stop."

I work her furiously at a steady pace, and I can feel her body tensing. It's not going to be much longer.

Regina screams out and her whole body bucks and shakes as her orgasm washes over her in waves upon waves.

I don't relent in my pace and I hold onto her as the aftershocks shimmer through her like a beam of light.

After a few moments, she settles down, trying to catch her breath. I stand up, looking down at her, a smile spreading across my face.

She looks at me with eyes that are wide and dilated.

"Well, goddamn," she says. "I'm as high as I've even been in my life. That was…I don't know what that was!"

She starts to giggle, and I laugh along with her.

"I'm glad you're pleased," I say.

"That's putting it mildly," she responds. "And now…I need more."

She gives me a wicked little grin and I nod.

"Yes ma'am," I say, and I pull a condom out of my wallet. I set it down on the nightstand and strip my pants off.

Her eyes stay on me the whole time, full of hunger and need.

"Fuck, you look good baby," she says to me.

As I pull my boxers off, my manhood springs free, fully hard, and erect. So hard that it fucking aches. I look down and see myself throbbing with my own pulse.

Regina's eyes grow wide when she gets a look at me, so ready for it.

"I *need* to take that into my mouth," she implores me, but I shake my head.

"Later. I need to be *in* you first. I can't wait any longer. Can I be in you, love?"

She lowers her chin, biting her lip and nods slowly.

"Yes baby. Take me. Be in me. Be *deep* in me. Now."

Regina lays back on the bed and spreads her lithe legs wide for me. With one hand, she cups her left breast, her other hand sliding down to her clit, gently teasing it.

"I'm ready for more. I'm so ready for you," she breathes.

I slide the condom down my engorged shaft and even that momentary bit of tightness feels good.

I climb onto the bed, placing myself above her, looking directly into her eyes.

"Are you ready?" I ask.

She doesn't reply, but merely nods with the slightest hint of a whimper.

Reaching down, I guide myself to her entrance, and I can feel the heat of her emanating off. Regina's hands slide down my sides and find their way to my ass, gripping it tightly.

"Now," she says, nodding. "I want it. Right fucking now. Give yourself to me."

And then, in one fluid motion, I plunge myself into her, all the way to the hilt.

We both gasp and moan at the same time.

I don't think I've ever felt anything as good as this in my entire life.

Chapter Twenty-Nine

REGINA

The second that Michael slides inside me, it feels like the entire world goes away and nothing exists but the two of us.

It is a moment of such exquisite pleasure, I find myself gasping, eyes growing wide, as he pushes his full length deep within.

"Oh..." I sputter, "oh good lord. Michael...oh Michael...I don't want you to ever exit me."

He nods furiously, his eyes closed, his face awash with the pleasure of it all.

"This is all I've ever wanted, here, with you," he moans out to me. And he means it. I reach out and touch his face and he presses his cheek into my hand.

"You belong here. In me," I say.

"Yes. Yes. Yes," he grunts out as he thrusts.

He rocks his hips back and forth, slowly at first. The friction and the tension are almost unbearable. It feels so good.

Michael opens his eyes and looks directly into mine. He opens his mouth to say something, but he's caught up in the moment so much, he can't get the words out.

"Shhh," I whisper, stroking his face. "I know. I know it, baby. Take what you need now. That's what I want. Take what you need."

I reach down to feel the strength of his legs as he pumps and rocks himself into me. His corded muscles feel like steel, so taut and so powerful. This is a man, through and through.

And he is mine.

I can feel the fullness of him in me, growing thicker, fuller. My eyes roll back in my head at the pleasure of it all. It's so good. It's so damn good.

"That's it, love…that's what I need right now…find that rhythm, find it with me," I pant out and he grunts in response.

He lowers his head to my breast, and I lift it up to meet his mouth. His lips wrap around my erect, aching nipple as he teases it with his tongue. Every flick, a little jolt of electricity shoots through me like a live wire.

I find myself whimpering in the pleasure of it all. Michael's thrusts become stronger, deeper, his need growing with every move.

I've already orgasmed once…another one is building again. I can't believe it. It's usually more difficult for me to come from penetration, but this…this is something altogether different.

"I need more," Michael says, looking at me with raw hunger that drove me wild.

"Then take more," I say, with a crooked smile on my face.

He reaches out then, pinning my wrists down, holding me in place.

"Oh no," I say in a gently sarcastic tone, "however will I get away?"

He grins at me then, a wicked little one and he drives into me harder, deeper.

"Fuck yes, baby," I groan. "Fucking take it."

Michael moves with abandon now, no pretense at softness or patience. Just pure, animal need. And I move my body to match him at every turn.

Our hips are coming together as one, bouncing off each other with power. I can feel myself soaking the sheets, I'm so wet. And he's harder than ever.

"Goddamn," he moans out, "it feels like I'm going to burst."

"Do it, baby," I say, "release it. Let it out. I want it. Give it to me. Now."

I didn't have long to wait. Michael's pattern changed, becoming even more urgent. I could feel him swelling inside me. It's amazing.

He looks at me, eyes wide and bright and he nods desperately.

"Yes, baby. Yes. Cum for me. Please. I need it. Please."

That is all it took. He moans loudly and starts thrusting forward, almost reflexively. His body shudders and he falls down onto me, the weight and heat of him feeling incredible.

I kiss him softly on his neck, tasting his sweat and smelling his musk. Michael's fingers find their way into my hair and he gives it a slight pull. I grin and pull back from him, increasing the tension.

"Regina," he finally says, coming up for air, "I've never felt anything like you. In all the days of my life."

He leans into me, kissing my mouth tenderly and I return it in kind.

"Nor have I, love. Nor have I."

He rolls to the side and pulls off the condom. Getting off the bed, he pads into the bathroom and I hear the running water of the sink and the flush of the toilet.

With a glass in his hand, Michael comes back to the bed, offering me the water. I take it, greedily gulping it down.

He laughs, as the water spills from the glass down my chin and onto my breasts.

"That's the luckiest water in the whole world," he says with a smile and leans down, licking it off my skin.

"Oh god," I moan. "Fuck, even *that* feels so damn good."

"It's *all* so damn good," he counters, and I have to agree.

He shifts down next to me on the bed and I can feel my hunger growing again already as I look at his naked body.

I start tracing my fingers on his side and he turns his head to look at me.

"What are you doing?" Michael says with a smirk.

"Just playing," I say innocently.

"Oh yeah? You're not done yet?"

"Honey, I'm *never* done," I say with a laugh. "So you'd better be ready to step up."

He turns onto his side, propping his head up on his hand.

"I'm always ready," he says cockily.

"We'll see about that," I say and reach down and take his manhood in my hand, stroking it slightly.

He issues a small groan, and I can feel him respond to my touch. I grip him a little harder and move a little faster.

"Regina…fuck…oh god…"

"That's right, baby, get harder for me. I need you again."

He swells in my hand almost instantly, growing full and thick, and now it's my turn. I flip him on his back and straddle him.

"I don't have any more condoms," he says softly.

I shake my head.

"Don't worry about it. I'm on the pill. And I need you again. Now."

I grasp him in my hands and guide him into me, slowly putting my full weight down on him.

"Fuck," I grunt and start rocking my hips on him.

Needless to say…the rest of the night was amazing.

Chapter Thirty

MICHAEL

My eyes are closed, and I draw in the deepest breath in history. Warm, blazing heat is radiating out from where she sits on top of me. It spreads from the core of me out to every inch of my body. As I breathe out, I open my eyes and look up at her.

She's the most beautiful thing I've ever seen. The afternoon light coming in from the closed blinds, frames her body in a daydream. As she pushes and pulls, grinding down on top of me, I feel helpless to do anything but my part. I grind my heels down into the bed and push up into her.

On and on, forward and back, until her breath quickens, and her moaning becomes more and more steady. I can feel the pressure building up, a rising momentum that's about to crash over us both. Her hands come down hard on my stomach, feeling my abs contract as I push into her with one last hard thrust.

We both come, breathing out simultaneously into the daylight of the bedroom. Her voice slows down to a honey-sweet calm as she climbs off me and tucks in next to me, under my armpit.

"Damn," I say. I feel like I'm in a dream.

"Damn," she replies. Her voice is smiling a hazy smile.

"Damn damn," I reply.

"Double damn," she says. And we are both chuckling.

The laugh dies down in the room, and it gets comfortably quiet. I raise my hand off the bed in slow motion. It feels like it weighs a ton. Her hand joins mine. Our fingers are lacing in and out of one another as they hover over the bed.

"How long 'til we can go again?" she says.

I grin at her. "That is the question, isn't it?"

Twice more on the bed. Once on the floor of the bedroom. Once in the kitchen as she was making us some toast. And finally, one last time in the chair back in the bedroom. We spend the day, crashing together like we are trying to exorcize the idea of one another out of our bodies.

I've been with many women in my life, but I can't remember the last time I felt this kind of wild animal hunger. Everything else in the world seems to have faded into a soft focus, and there's only this house, our bodies, her skin, her taste, her smell. I feel like I'm twenty years old again.

When we're done on the chair, she folds into me. She sits on my lap, facing me. I breathe a deep, tired sigh, and she wraps her arms around my neck and rests down on top of me.

"I can't help but notice the sun's gone down," she says.

"Oh, wow. It has. What time is it?" I ask.

"You know … I'm not really wearing my watch," she says. I chuckle.

"Yeah, we're not wearing much right now."

"Haven't been for a while, it seems," she agrees.

My stomach grumbles. Reality is setting back in.

"Oh man. Are you hungry?" I ask.

"Starving," she replies. "Let's get back in that kitchen and cook up some dinner."

"Yes, please," I say.

She climbs off me and scrambles around the floor gracefully, finding her clothes and plucking them back onto her incredible body piece by piece. I do the same, grabbing my pants and under-shirt.

"Alright," I say.

"Off to the kitchen," she says, walking out of the bedroom.

Then, turning around and poking her finger into my chest she says, "And hey. No *funny business* in the kitchen, okay? If we get … *distracted* … we're never gonna finish cooking anything."

"Well," I say, "we could always order delivery."

She purses her lips into a wry smile, reaches up to my face and pulls me into her for a kiss. "Be good," she says.

"Okay, okay," I say, "I promise."

As we eat dinner, we're quiet. We carve up our food and bring it to our mouths to feed like a couple of high school athletes exhausted by a day of hard practice.

It's strange, I'm not used to passing time in this kind of quiet. The kind of quiet where minutes pass, and the fact that you might not have anything to say doesn't feel tense or upsetting. It's comfortable.

Regina looks up from her plate and meets my eyes. A smile slowly blooms on her face. And we chuckle under our breath at each other, like we have a secret.

"Can I say something?" I ask.

"Oh, if you *must*," she says.

"Well, I've been thinking," I say.

"Have you? Is that what you've been doing all day?" she says.

I laugh and shake my head. "I'm very good at multitasking."

"So I've noticed," she says.

"But seriously. I've been thinking that maybe we could come to an agreement about the estate."

She lets down the guard of her humor. Lifting her chin up to take in the serious information, she looks at me straight on.

"What kind of agreement?" she asks.

"Call it a truce," I say. "I'm thinking maybe I can handle the estate on my own. If I take that off your plate, you can focus on the finances of the bakery."

"I don't know," she says. I can tell that she's gone back into her head now, weighing the options, trying to figure out just how much she can trust me with all this.

"Come on," I say, "We've been at each other's throats since the minute I got here. You're stressed. It's too much at once. Let me carry some of it."

"I suppose it would feel good to just have *one* stressful mess to sort out instead of two," she says. "I guess I could let you take the lead on the estate."

I shrug and lift a forkful of food up to my mouth.

"You did call us for help, after all," I say.

"You're right," she says, "and thank goodness for that."

The day comes to an end, and the night air is thick and silent out the window. We lie next to each other in the bed. Her leg is draped over me. We're wrapped up in each other's arms. Quiet.

I could get used to this.

Chapter Thirty-One

REGINA

"Okay, I'm leaving for the bakery," I call upstairs as I stand in my coat near the front door.

"Great, have a good time," Michael says, appearing at the top of the stairs. He's freshly showered, with just a towel wrapped around his waist. Seeing his still-wet body, I consider 'calling out sick' and forcing him back into bed.

You've done enough of that, I tell myself. *Now duty calls.*

Thinking of our now separate assignments, my eyes can't help but slide in the direction of the office, where all Mama's paperwork sits on the desk.

Michael catches the look. "I've got this, just like we talked about, remember?" he says gently.

"I know. Okay. See you later."

I hurry out the door before I can second-guess myself any further.

The drive from the house to the bakery is one I could do in my sleep. It requires no thought on my part, meaning my brain is free to linger on other things. Of course it chooses to linger on Michael.

I'm falling for a guy that lives in Chicago. There is little doubt in my mind that he is going *back* to Chicago as soon as things are wrapped up here. The fact that he is now going to be working without my interrupting – or sexually distracting – him probably means his pace will increase exponentially. Then he'll be gone. And I'll still be here.

Alone. Effectively unemployed. And Mama gone.

They say, 'you can never go home again'. It's not exactly true. Home is always there, and you can always get to it. The problem is, you can never go home again and have it be the same as it used to be. And you're never the same when you return home, either. That can be great when things are going well. It can be hell when you've retreated there with your tail between your legs.

There's no chance me and this place can offer Michael anything that would convince him to stay, I think, as the town passes by my windows.

I turn that part of my brain off as I pull into the bakery's parking lot and turn off the car engine.

Bridgid looks confused when she sees me walk through Muffin Top's doors. Her confusion turns into a bit of alarm when she sees me slip around behind the counter and put on an apron.

"Have I stepped into some kind of alternate universe?" she asks. "What's going on here?"

I pour myself a coffee from the pot she's got on the warmer, then fill her in. At first, I try to make it seem like Michael and I just came to this agreement as two intelligent, sane professional people. But as I tell her about it, the secret of our affair becomes too much to contain and I let some of that slip as well.

As I wrap it up, Bridgid just stares at me with a look I can't make out. "What's that face?" I ask.

"Oh," she says, recovering. "I'm sorry. Did I not make a surprise face? I meant to make a surprise face." With an exaggerated manner, she widens her eyes and lets her jaw drop.

"Ha-ha," I intone flatly. "So everyone saw it coming but me."

"Emphasis on the word —"

"Don't," I warn her with a smile. "Not in Mama's bakery." Bridgid pulls her lips together tight. "Okay," I say, changing the subject, "fill me in on the way you're doing things, now."

Bridgid starts walking me through the changes and improvements she's made to the bakery. I have to admit, despite the ways we clashed before, she's been making smart choices. Among them is a modern **POS** system for the register. It takes me a few tries to figure out how the Point-of-Sale program works, but I finally get the hang of it.

After I make a successful test transaction, I close the register drawer and discover Bridgid's now beaming at me with tears in her eyes. "Aw, come on, it didn't take me *that* long to figure it out," I say.

Bridgid suddenly wraps her arms around my neck and pulls me in for a tight hug, nearly strangling me. "I'm just so happy you're here," she says as I feel a tear drop onto my shoulder. She takes a deep breath as she pulls away, wiping at her eyes. "If Mama could see us now."

"The shock'd kill her all over again."

Bridgid slaps me playfully on the arm. Then we're interrupted by a customer. Bridgid 'allows' me to take care of him and I get through the transaction without giving him the wrong change, which I count as a definite win.

As the customer leaves and Bridgid gently claps in my direction, I can't help but feel some sense of reservation. It wasn't that long ago that Bridgid and I were completely at odds over the bakery going under. Still, I know I won't be able to forgive myself if I don't at least *try* to make this work.

I guess that's something else I can be grateful to Michael for. His insistence on tackling the finances alone is giving me the opportunity to take working with Bridgid at the bakery for a test drive.

While my stomach knots itself at the thought that I'm no longer directly involved in the finalization of Mama's paperwork, I decide to find whatever joy I can here in her bakery.

It still smells like Mama. I remember she used to come home every day from here smelling like her cookies and cupcakes. That same sweet aroma surrounds me and Bridgid now, as though Mama is wrapping us up in a warm hug.

Okay, Mama, I think, *this is for you as much as it is for me.*

A moment later, the morning rush comes bursting through and Bridgid and I are in a balletic swirl of activity, moving with ease and efficiency as if we'd be doing it all our lives.

Chapter Thirty-Two

MICHAEL

Now this is more like it, I tell myself as I get to work on Regina's mother's finances. In the first hour of my solo embarkation on the day's endeavors, I've already made excellent headway.

I try not to think about how empty the office feels without Regina. I try not to think about how I'm a stranger in the house of a dead woman whose daughter I've spent the last twenty-four hours passionately making love to.

To fill the quiet, I open up a music app on my phone and play some tunes. Unfortunately, every song the app plays seems to be a love song or one about sex or something sexual that just puts me in mind of Regina, arousing and distracting me yet again.

It's not just that I'm missing her body, though. I miss her company. I even miss her constant nagging at me, and our bickering. I realize now, it was foreplay masked as fighting. Despite how crazy she is, she is also a woman full of life and fight and power.

I think of the girls I've been with back in Chicago. All corporate, all towing the company line, all of their personal life sectioned off and packaged away for the sake of 'making it' in business.

Not Regina. She's all herself, operating on all cylinders, all the time. I guess that's why she's ended up back here without a job. She's too much raw female energy for them to take in the corporate rat race.

I could take it, though.

Despite my mind wandering to thoughts of her, without any of Regina's tangible distractions, I start flying through Mama's paperwork. I've already closed out accounts that were taking forever for me to get through before. Some of the estate finances are finally becoming clear. I can probably wrap this up in no time, at this rate.

Around mid-day, I stop for lunch. There are leftovers in the fridge, which is what I'd been planning to eat. That way I can get something in me quick, then dive back into the accounts.

Except, I think, *what's the rush, really? The office knows what I'm doing out here. I'm being paid. I don't have any accounts back in Chicago that are incredibly pressing. No reason not to take advantage of where you are and enjoy a leisurely lunch.*

So I pop on over to Billy Bob's BBQ, thinking I'll have a seat, grab a sandwich and maybe even a beer.

Once I get there, though, an even better thought occurs to me. "Can I do take-out?" I ask the hostess.

"Sure. Just head on over to the counter."

I do. A jovial, overweight guy in a BBQ-stained white apron and a baseball cap sporting the joint's logo greets me. He pulls a pen out from behind his ear and grabs a grease-stained order pad. "What can I get you?"

I look up at the menu board. I settle on a half-pound of brisket, half-pound of sausage and medium sides of mac and cheese and collard greens. Then I have him throw in a few bottled sodas, as well.

Fifteen minutes later, he passes an overstuffed brown bag across the counter to me. He rings up my credit card and I drop some cash in the old-school coffee can that acts as the tip jar.

"Hey, what's your name?" I ask the guy.

"Liam," he tells me, and extends his paw for a shake.

"I'm Michael, nice to meet you," I say, shaking his hand. Then I head out with my bag, giving a wave and smile to the hostess as I leave.

It's not until I'm in my car that I wonder what the hell I did that for. *Getting to know the names of the folks at the local BBQ spot? It's like you were trying to go native or something.* I quickly shake the thought out of my head and drive over to the bakery.

"Special delivery," I say as I make my way inside, holding the bag aloft. "Holy moly, it smells *amazing* in here."

Regina looks surprised to see me. Bridgid gives me a sly smile. Guess the cat's out of the bag there. Whatever. I try to play it nonchalant.

"I was making good headway," I explain, "so I decided we could all have some lunch together."

"Fantastic," Bridgid says.

Regina continues to just stare at me from behind the counter.

"Um… I'll get us plates and stuff," Bridgid offers and slips into the kitchen.

"Is it all right I came by?" I ask Regina hesitantly.

"Yeah. Yeah, it's great." She finally smiles and I give a sigh of relief.

"C'mere," I say to her.

"Why?"

"Just c'mere." I go to the counter and gesture for her to lean forward. She does. I wipe away the little bit of powder on her nose. She looks down, embarrassed. I sneak a quick peck on her lips before Bridgid pops back out of the kitchen, loudly announcing her return as if she knew what might be going on.

"Let's dig in," I say loudly in return so as to cover my blushing.

As we sit at one of the bakery's tables and divvy up the amazing BBQ, I study Regina's face and attitude. She eats with gusto. There's a smile on her face. "Someone seems to be enjoying their day," I say.

"We've been having a great time," Bridgid offers, "haven't we?"

"Yeah, it's been OK," Regina says. She tries to play it cool, but her smile is wide, revealing her gleaming white teeth. Then she turns to me and looks serious again. "What about the finances?"

"Everything's under control," I say, my mouth full of smoky brisket.

But Regina sets down her fork and starts in on me. Did I remember this, am I going to make sure I check on that, it's important that I contact so-and-so regarding the other thing.

"Hey, Regina, I've got it," I finally say as definitively as I can.

She backs off, pushes some collard greens around with her fork. "Right, right, of course." Then she hops out of her chair. "Who wants some dessert? I can get us something for free. I happen to be tight with the owner."

As she goes to grab us something from the dessert case, I settle back and take a pull off my bottle of soda. As I enjoy the feel of the BBQ in my belly and the aroma of the sweet treats Regina – in all her long, dark, and beautiful glory – delivers to the table, I have another thought.

This could be a nice life.

Chapter Thirty-Three

REGINA

"Here you go, Kyle, two blueberry muffins and a large coffee, one cream, two sugars," I say, passing the paper bag of pastries and the cup of coffee over to Kyle. He grins and presses some cash into an already overflowing tip jar.

"Bridgid," Kyle calls out to my sister, who's busy grabbing some danishes for another customer, "where'd you find this lovely lady?"

"She was just wandering around outside, and I told her if she wasn't going anywhere, she might as well make herself useful," Regina jokes. "I had no idea she'd be so good at it!"

"See you tomorrow, Kyle?" I ask as he heads out the door.

"Where else could I go?"

I give him one last smile and wave. It's only been a few days, but I'm already familiar with most of our regulars and their orders. Kyle didn't even have to open his mouth. I'd rung him up and gotten his things together by the time he got to the front of the line. The delight people have in Bridgid and I knowing what they need is contagious. It makes the hard work seem like fun.

The fun is due to more than just the customers, though.

Bridgid and I dance through the day as much as we do hustle to get our customers satisfied. The bakery radio plays a streaming station of music we've set to be a mix of mine and Bridgid's favorites mixed with the old school tunes Mama used to love. Now and again, we treat our customers to an impromptu concert, singing along to the music we love.

Our nascent partnership is turning out to be more enjoyable than I could have ever foreseen. I don't know exactly why that is. Maybe it's the influence of Joel. Maybe it's that she's coming into her own as a young woman. Maybe it's that the stress of losing the bakery is behind us. Whatever the reason, Bridgid is way more fun than I remember her to be.

Of course, it's also possible that *I'm* more fun than I used to be. Maybe some of that is the influence of Michael. There's no denying that coming home to him every evening, making love to him every night, and waking up in his arms every morning is filling me with positive vibes.

He pops by the bakery at 2pm everyday, which is when we tend to have a lull in business, and forces Bridgid and I to take a break. He brings us an array of dishes from some of the best places in town. The three of us enjoy our meal like we were family. Every now and again, I sort of step outside myself and watch the proceedings with wonder. *Who are these happy people?* I think. *Is that my sister? Is that me? Is that my…*

My what?

When I hit that question, I let things be. I tell myself that things are sweet the way they are and questioning it can only make them go sour.

After lunch, Michael heads back to the house to work on the finances. Bridgid and I get ready for that late-afternoon rush. Then it's time for end-of- day duties, cleaning up, bagging the left-over pastries and bread for the food bank that will pick them up, closing out the register, splitting the mound of cash in the tip jar with Bridgid, and locking up.

Amid all this routine, I hardly ever think of the job that I lost, the world I left behind. Maybe that's because I'm feeling something that I never really felt when I was in the fast-paced, dog-eat-dog business world:

Contentment.

Regina and I usually lock up just as the sun has started to set. Joel's car is always waiting in the parking lot for Bridgid. Sometimes I stop and chat with him through the driver's side window until Bridgid tells us "gossips" that she's hungry for dinner and Joel shrugs at me and drives off.

Then it's home to Mama's house, where Michael is waiting for me. Usually, he's got candles lit on the table and something cooking on the stove.

"I've taken to looking up interesting recipes on the internet," he tells me as he makes me taste whatever it is he's preparing for the night. "I never have time to cook back in Chicago. I'm enjoying this."

"Mm-hm," I tease, invariably loving whatever he's made, "so what you're saying is, without me to put your nose to the grindstone, you waste your time surfing the web instead of working on Mama's finances."

"And don't forget," he teases back, putting his arm around my waist and pulling me in close, "you're billing me by the hour."

"You're lucky you're hot," I tell him, "or I'd fire your ass."

Instead, I slap it. Sometimes we get so wrapped up in one another that whatever's on the stove starts boiling over. I'm afraid our foreplay has led to more than one meal being burned.

At night, in bed, we make passionate love. His body atop mine feels like a sensual blanket, comfortable and exciting all at the same time. When I take him inside me, he excites a passion in me unlike anything I've ever felt. When we cum together, it's like there is no division between us. We're united in ecstasy that lasts until the morning when we wake up and give each other still-sleepy kisses.

These are days that last forever and go by too quickly. They're like one unending summer evening trapped in a time capsule and I could languish in them for the rest of my life. These are days that I want to last forever.

Each night, however, while Michael's doing the dishes or brushing his teeth, I slip into the office and check how his work is progressing. The stack of unfinished paperwork gets smaller every day. The completed and filed-away pile keeps growing taller.

It's only a matter of time before he returns to Chicago.

I remind myself that these days are *not* captured in a time capsule. They are limited. And so, as much as I would like to let myself go and give my emotions to Michael for free reign, I know I must guard myself against the inevitable.

Chapter Thirty-Four

MICHAEL

"Wait a minute," says the bank manager I'm on the phone with. "Didn't I just talk to you yesterday about this same account?"

"Um, yeah," I stammer, "just, I was dotting my *I*s and crossing my *T*s, y'know, so I thought I'd just, um, double-check."

"Well, the answer's the same as it was yesterday," he says, clearly annoyed by me.

"Right, right, great, thanks so much," I say hurriedly and hang up.

I'm embarrassed. The guy's absolutely right, of course, I *did* just call him with the same question yesterday. Just like the other company I called twice this morning, again pretending to just be 'double checking'.

What's really going on is that I'm stalling, plain and simple. The estate's affairs are nearly settled. And once they are, it'll be time for me to go back to Chicago.

Which means it'll be time for me to leave Regina.

I would like to pretend that there's nothing going on between us. That this is just a fling, like a few others I've had in the past. Physical. Maybe with that added bit of passion that can get thrown into the mix when you know your time is short. Like a summer love that is able to an approximation of love precisely because you know you'll both soon be on planes to separate places, never to see each other again, so why not let yourselves pretend?

It would be nice if what I was feeling was just that. My heart, my gut, and my brain all tell me that it's way more complicated – and fulfilling – than that.

Except, I've never felt this way about a woman before. I even have a feeling that she feels something for me, too.

It'd be easier if there were no emotions involved. I could wrap up the estate, we could have one more night in bed together, and I could be on my way with an experience to tell the guys about over beers sometime.

But every time I think of getting back on a plane to Chicago, I feel an ache. Every time I imagine my life back in the windy city without Regina in it, I feel a void.

I need to know. Need to test the waters and see if going back to Chicago might just be the dumbest thing I could ever do.

It's with that in mind that I decide to forego lunch with the sisters today and have a little date just with Regina.

Digging around in the basement, Regina's Mama's spirit comes through for me and I find, tucked away in a corner, a vintage, wicker picnic basket. I dust it off and wipe it out, then head to the grocery store. I stock up on picnic items – cheese and crackers, summer sausage, and some strawberries for dessert.

I swing by the bakery at my usual time. When I get there, I don't immediately get out of the car, however. For some weird reason, I actually feel nervous. Like I'm a kid about to ask a girl out on a date for the first time. It's ridiculous. Regina and I have already made love countless times. Why does this feel different?

Because it is *different, you dolt,* I tell myself. *Even if you're not willing to admit it to her, at least admit it to yourself. You're here today with a different kind of hope.*

I take one more deep breath, then pop out of the car and into the bakery.

Regina is finishing up with a customer. She catches my eye and gives me a half-smile before quickly returning her attention to the elderly lady grabbing her weekly fix of cookies. The elderly lady smiles at me as she leaves and I say, "Thanks for coming in," as though I'm somehow attached to the place.

Or wish I was.

I stare at my feet, embarrassed, and hope Regina didn't see that. What a give-away that would be, and I'm not ready to be that transparent. Yet.

When I look up, Regina is taking off her apron and dropping it on the counter. She calls into the kitchen, "Bee? Lunch is here."

I wince. "Actually," I say as Bridgid comes racing out, "um, I was hoping *we* could just do lunch. The two of us, I mean." I gesture between myself and Regina.

"We're just going to sit here and eat in front of her?" Regina asks.

"No, uh, I thought we could, um, go *out*. I've got a picnic."

"I don't know…" Regina says, glancing back at Bridgid.

"It's not good for you to be cooped up inside all day on your feet," I offer. "You've been busting your butt. You deserve a little time in the sunshine." I can see Regina is not convinced. I turn to Bridgid and say, "You don't mind. Right?"

"You know, she *could* use some sun," Bridgid says slowly, a smile creeping over her face.

"What about you?" Regina asks.

"I'll manage," Bridgid insists. "You go and have your little picnic."

Regina continues to hesitate. Then, finally, she says to her sister, "We'll bring you something on the way back."

"Sure, take your time," Bridgid says, waving us out of the bakery.

I hold the door open for Regina and we head out to the car. Like a dork, I rush ahead of her and open the passenger side door. "My lady," I say with mock formality.

"Why thank you, kind sir," she says. She steps one foot in the car, then pauses. She studies me for a moment. I try to keep my face pleasantly neutral. Then she slips into the seat and I close the door after her.

When I hop into the driver's side, Regina has the picnic basket on her lap and is staring at it like it's an ancient artifact. "Mama's picnic basket," she exclaims, smiling. "I haven't seen this since I was a little girl…"

I give her a grin, feeling like things are off to a great start. Then I put the car in gear and head out for the local park.

As I drive, Regina takes my hand. She holds it the whole way there.

Chapter Thirty-Five

REGINA

There are some days that seem like they are made for a drive. A bright, clean sun, a cool, comfortable breeze and all the time in the world.

This is one of those days. And as Michael drives along, it feels good to open the window and let the air brush against my skin and in my face. It makes me feel alive in the best way.

Michael had been coy when he picked me up and still isn't telling me what the plan is. But that's okay. I can roll with it, just like the best of them.

"How you doin?" he says, with a smile in his voice.

I turn to him with a grin.

"I'm doing very well, thank you. Although I'm excited to see what our ultimate destination is going to be."

He laughs at that and I love hearing the sound of it.

"Hang tight, kid. We're going to be there soon. I promise."

We keep moving ahead and pretty soon, I see a turn that I recognize.

"Michael! You're taking me to my park!"

He laughs again and nods.

"I'm not sure that it's exactly 'yours', but I know how much you love it. And I thought, with a day like this ahead of us, it was a good time to enjoy it."

I smile from ear to ear.

"I couldn't agree with you more. I don't think this is a route I'd ever taken here before."

"No indeed," he says. "I tried to find one that was a little unfamiliar, so it could be more of a surprise."

"Well done, Magellan," I say, giving him a playful shove on the shoulder. Then he gives me that laugh again.

I marvel to myself at how simple and easy things always seem to be with us. The chemistry we share is undeniable. And it feels so damn good.

Michael pulls into the park's lot and we find a spot. It's fairly crowded, which makes perfect sense, given what kind of day it is.

"Now," he says with a grin, "time for the provisions."

We get out and he pops the trunk and produces an absolutely enormous picnic basket. The thing was huge.

"What did you bring for lunch? The whole supermarket?"

"Hey," he says lightly, "I was a Boy Scout. Gotta be prepared, ya know. Who knows what we may need?"

"I like it. Good thinking," I reply, leaning in to give him a quick kiss on the cheek.

Michael unloads the basket, props it on his broad shoulders and off we go into the park, looking for a little spot to call our own.

There are lots of families out, couples, people walking their dogs and friends tossing frisbees and footballs around. Seems like I'm not the only one who is feeling a little more alive today.

We find a place under a couple trees, just off from the main field. No one else over here but us. It's perfect.

Michael puts the basket down and cracks it open. To my delight, he pulls out sandwiches, a huge salad, fruit, cheese and crackers, a bottle of white wine and a bottle of sparkling water. Basically everything that you could want for an outdoor meal.

"Well," I say with enthusiasm, "this is pretty damn great."

"I aim to please," Michael says. "Don't stand on ceremony. Dig in! Get it while the getting is good!"

He didn't need to tell me twice. I dish myself some salad and grab a sandwich while he opens the wine and pours us each a glass.

I take mine and he offers his for a toast.

"Here's to sunshine and beautiful days," he says.

For some reason, the simplicity of that moves me deeply and I find myself almost in tears.

"Amen," I reply, and we clink our glasses.

Michael grabs an apple and starts chowing down on it, like he'd never eaten in his life.

"Mmm," he says, "why does food outside just *taste* better?"

"I don't know," I answer, "but maybe it's because when we're all outside, on days like this…we all feel free. And everything is better when you're feeling free."

He looks at me then, deep into my eyes and then nods.

"That's right, Regina. That's completely right."

He leans in then and kisses me suddenly and it fills me with a delight and a shiver that shoots through my whole body.

Michael breaks from me, smiles warmly and then picks up a sandwich and takes an absurdly large bite, making me laugh yet again.

That's when I feel it.

There's this…pang…somewhere far inside my chest, my torso. It's an ache and it's *strong*. But it's not the kind that hurts. Just the opposite, in fact.

It feels like I'm being filled with light.

I'm in love with him. I'm in love with Michael.

I know it as sure as I'm sitting here.

It's not a feeling that I've had before. Not really. But it's hitting me so strong that I can't imagine that it's anything else.

I look at Michael and see he's looking intently at me.

"Hey," he says concerned, "you okay? You got awfully quiet there. It's like you went away."

I shake myself out of it. The feeling is threatening to overwhelm me and if I'm not careful, I could drown in it. And I don't know that this is the time to tell Michael about how I'm feeling.

"Sorry, no, I'm here. I promise. I was just…I was just so enjoying myself. And I was reflecting on that. I feel lucky, you know? Lucky to be having a day like this with you."

Michael smiles slowly and warmly at that and he nods his head.

"I know *exactly* what you mean. I feel the same way. Now, listen, don't punk out on me. There's a ton of food here and I expect you to take your full share!"

I give him a mock salute.

"Aye-aye, captain," I say, and he chuckles, pouring us some more wine.

But I can feel a worry building somewhere in the back of my brain.

What am I going to do when Michael has to leave? Because he's going to be taking part of me with him, whether he likes it or not.

Chapter Thirty-Six

Maybe I'm overcompensating. Maybe it's because Regina's been so quiet during lunch, and her reticence continues on the car ride back to the bakery. Maybe that's why I can't seem to shut up.

"Look at this," I say, for example, as we pass a little open-air market, pointing to a woman standing behind a table covered in souvenir mugs. "Look at all those Texas mugs. That's all that woman sells. *Texas mugs*. Three-hundred-and-sixty-five days a year. Think how creative you have to be to make that many different kinds of mugs out of a logo that's just one lone star."

I grin at my, admittedly, dad-esque joke. Regina seems not to hear it. She just stares absentmindedly out the window, biting a thumbnail.

Not knowing what else to do, I blabber on, saying, "I wonder if she ever tries to play around with the slogan, at least? Like, 'Don't *jest* with Texas'? 'Don't *zest* with Texas…' 'Don't *obsess* in Texas'? Or maybe it's best not to mess with 'don't mess with Texas'?"

I do a little rim-shot off the steering wheel, but she still seems out of it. Her silence is deafening. Not that she laughs at all my dumb jokes, but when she doesn't, she usually is giving me an earful about why the joke is so stupid.

In the time we've been together, half the fun of my making a bad joke has been – not the joke itself – but her inevitably over-the-top reaction to the inherent badness of it.

You're really in a predicament with a girl, I think, when you take her not bothering to heckle you as a sign of trouble.

I finally give over to the awkwardness and drive the rest of the way in silence. When we pull up to the bakery, any thoughts I might've had about ending this little picnic date with a make-out session are well put to rest. Seated in my tiny rental, there's less than two feet between us. It feels like it stretches on for miles.

Instead of a luxurious kiss on her mouth to say goodbye, I give her a quick peck on the cheek. She gives me a tight-lipped smile in response, making me feel like even the peck was me being pushy. Her behavior makes it hard to believe our bodies were ever close to each other, let alone touching, let alone *joined*.

Still, as she wanders into the shop, I can't help but watch her ass as she walks. My mind might have read that I was being given the cold shoulder, but my body was not picking up the same signals. It was left wondering what I was doing letting that gorgeous woman out of my car with just a peck to speak of.

I had to sort of grin at myself. Hard to believe, after how much we'd enjoyed each other of late, that I still felt like I couldn't get enough of her.

My erection was still semi-hard when I got back to the house. I tried to ignore the ache inside me and instead set my brain on the paperwork in the office. On the other hand, there wasn't that much left to do. In fact, what would be the harm if I took the afternoon off?

Maybe I could take care of myself and then when Regina got home, I could match her chilly-ness. Not need to touch her, kiss her, be inside of her. In fact, what would be the harm if I slowed down and let the work take a few more days, even…?

No.

The word bust through my thoughts like a gunshot. And the bullet deflated the fantasy-balloon that I realized I'd been creating. A fantasy about this house. A fantasy that Regina and I could have some sort of life together, maybe. A fantasy that included the laughable idea that I'd live in fucking *Texas,* of all places. What a weird little dream to have concocted!

More like con-*cock*-ted. Because that's clearly what I'd been thinking with, right? This was not a *reasonable* fantasy.

Except, if it was so ridiculous, how come letting that fantasy fall to the ground made something in my chest feel heavy and leaden? As though the bullet had torn more than the fantasy-balloon? Had left a hole somewhere else?

"You know what they call that?" I ask out loud to myself, staring at the ceiling. "They call that: 'Getting Too Attached'." I push the mouse on the desk, waking up the computer monitor. "And you know what the remedy for Getting Too Attached is?" I ask myself again. "Work. Hard. Work."

With a renewed vigor, I open up the financial programs on the computer at the same time as I sit down. I start flying, clicking boxes, entering numbers, letting the computer do its microprocessor-speed math. As I click and type, two things become very clear to me, all at once.

One, I need to get through this estate paperwork and wrap things up as quickly as possible. That way, there is no time for Regina or I to make a mistake. The sooner I wrap up, the less likely it is that one of us will say or do something that cannot be taken back. Or, if we do, there won't be a lot of time to live in discomfort before I will be out of here.

Yes: *out of here.*

Because two, my life is back in Chicago. Which is where I need to get to as quickly as possible.

I start typing up an email to the lawyer. *"Attaching a lot of forms to this one,"* I write. *"Sorry. Getting a lot done all at once, here."*

There are so many documents that I end up needing to send half the attachments as a second email. I try not to think about the reason I've let so many unsent documents pile up. Can't be because I was stalling or anything like that, what reason would I have to do that, right…?

Anyway, they get sent.

Two hours later, when I stand up from the desk, nearly all of Mama's financial life has been settled and wrapped up. All that's missing is the tiny bow.

Then I can bow out.

Chapter Thirty-Seven

REGINA

A surprise greets me when I step in the house that evening. Michael's suitcases are sitting by the door, all packed and ready to go. A panic shoots through me. My throat tightens up and I have this irrational fear that he's already gone, fled from me, couldn't get away quick enough and is planning on sending someone to pick up his bags later or something like that –

Then I hear him in the kitchen.

I take a deep breath, tell my heart to get out of my throat and back in my chest where it belongs. Then I fix my face back to something neutral and make my way to where he's preparing dinner. For a moment, he doesn't see me, and I just watch him.

He's leaning over the stove, tasting whatever he's got going in the big pot there. And he's wiggling his butt to the song he's humming to himself. He's got one of Mama's aprons on, which makes him look cute enough to take a bite out of.

Had my legs not turned to lead when I saw the suitcases, maybe I would do just that. Sneak over to him, kiss him, run my hands along his body, feel the way he responds… But I can't stop thinking about the suitcases.

I lean against the doorway into the kitchen and he becomes aware of me. He does a little double-take, stopping mid-hum and straightening up. "Oh, hey."

"Oh hey," I say back, my tone restrained.

He picks up on it. "So, I'm all packed."

"Yeah, I saw that."

He hesitates just a moment. Then, as if Mama's business were the only thing we had in common, he says, "The estates all settled. Just needs a few signatures from you and Bridgid and it's good to go."

"And you're good to go, too, it looks like."

"Yeah." He hesitates again. It might be my imagination, but I think there's a touch of regret or embarrassment in his voice when he adds, "I'm heading back to Chicago in the morning."

For a moment, I think that an earthquake hits the house right as those words leave his mouth. It's just my legs shaking, though. I try to get a grip on them.

We both stand still, the distance between us across the kitchen suddenly feeling like it's a million miles. Each of us waits for the other to say what we're hoping to hear. At least, I'm hoping that's what he's waiting for, since it's definitely what I'm waiting for.

Neither of us says anything, though.

Eventually, he breaks the silence and gestures at the pot on the stove. "I finished everything up right after we got back from the park. Which gave me time to kill. I've always wanted to make homemade bolognese. But it's not really the sort of thing you make for just yourself." He looks at me out of the corner of his eye.

I don't move.

"And, anyway," he goes on, "I thought we deserved a nice last meal. To celebrate all the work we accomplished." He hesitates again.

Again, I don't respond. But now the words *last meal* bounce around in my brain like a bullet ricocheting around inside a small metal room, punching holes in everything in its path.

"And," he wraps up, "I grabbed us a fantastic bottle of wine." He holds up a bottle of Barbaresco like he's a model on a game show presenting a prize. "You, uh, you want to pour?" he asks me.

He extends the bottle of red wine and a corkscrew out to me; a questioning look on his face. I know what his ask really means. *Do I agree? Is this to be our last meal? Is it over?*

I take the bottle. I open it. I pour.

I can feel my heart crack in two as I pour. It takes all my concentration to keep my hands from shaking and spilling wine everywhere. It takes all my focus to keep from bursting out in tears. *Be strong, Regina,* I tell myself. *If this is our last night together, then let it be a nice one.*

We sit down to eat. The bolognese is delicious, rich and full of flavor. His pride over it makes me laugh despite my mood. Seeing me smile, he's encouraged to keep joking around. He tells me about the pasta his mom used to make – "Basically hamburger meat and ketchup over elbow noodles" – but as he talks a part of me wishes he would just leave already.

Grab your suitcases and go! I think about shouting at him. I envision grabbing him by the lapel and tossing him out the door, throwing the bags out after him. Wouldn't that be the best thing? Rip the band-aid right off. The quicker he's gone, the quicker I can be left alone to wallow in my self-pity.

Except that's not fair to him. I can't be upset that he's all packed up. Why should I expect him to stay? What have

I done to show him my feelings? Nagged him about paperwork? Teased him about the lunches he brings to the bakery?

We've slept together. We've made love. But there's a big difference between actions and words. Sometimes, when it comes to love, words really *do* speak louder. A touch isn't enough to make someone upend his life for you. A kiss is not really the same as asking someone to stay.

And I've never said the words. Never told him what was in my heart.

Because you assumed, he felt the same way, a voice in my head tells me.

Which he obviously doesn't. If he loved you back, he wouldn't have packed his bags. He'd be looking for a reason to stay. He wouldn't be referring to this bolognese as our 'last meal'.

I have to face the truth: I'm alone in my feelings for him.

So just enjoy this night, I tell myself. *Enjoy these final moments with him. Cherish it one last time, girl.*

Then let him go.

Chapter Thirty-Eight

MICHAEL

Before falling asleep, I had set my alarm on vibrate only and put it beside me on the bed, not even the nightstand. I didn't want it to go off and wake up Regina. I wanted to be able to slip away.

When it does start to vibrate on the mattress, the sun is barely up but I've already been awake for hours. I slept in fits and starts, my mind was racing with all sorts of thoughts, all of them running a track centered around one subject only:

Regina.

Beautiful, luscious Regina, still naked and asleep in bed beside me. The top sheet has come down a little bit in the night, exposing her full dark breasts with their bright pink nipples.

Last night was amazing. Our lovemaking had been sweet, gentle, extended. A slow passion that went beyond sex, went beyond our orgasms. It had been infused with a kind of intensity I thought only existed in the movies.

As I watch her breasts gently rise and fall with her sleeping breaths, I recall a certain part of last night in vivid detail.

I'd sat with my legs crossed, her straddling my lap with her legs wrapped tightly around my waist as I went deep inside her. She rocked her hips slightly as we sat there, moving just enough for us both to feel that inner connection, inwardly tightening her muscles around me and releasing, sending little thrills of joy through me.

While she did that, we kissed gently, softly, at times our lips barely grazing. Meanwhile, our fingertips brushed along every inch of one another's skin. It was like we were drawing each other. Like our bodies didn't exist until we touched that patch of skin and then it sprang into beautiful existence. All the while, our limbs were entangled as I pressed so far into her that there was no telling where one of us ended and the other began…

Well. It was easy to tell, now. I was leaving, after all.

As I brushed my teeth, I tried to ignore the pain in my chest. I try to pretend it's just heartburn from the bolognese last night.

As I showered, another moment from the previous night hits me. It's as we were like that, sitting up, and I'd taken her face in my hand. My white skin bathed in moonlight pressed against her beautiful black face. My thumb gently arcing across her lips before sliding down her body. My mouth on her breasts as my thumb worked softly on her clit, until she came for the first time, and as she moaned my name, our eyes met and I nearly said it, nearly told her how I felt.

But I didn't. And then we were on to a new position and the words slipped from my mind as she ground her hips round my cock and brought me to new levels of pleasure…

Next thing I know, I'm dressed, with my toiletry bag in hand. I try to look around and see if there's something in the bedroom that I've forgotten to pack, but that stalling tactic only eats up a few minutes.

I look again at Regina, asleep in bed. One of her long legs has slipped out from under the blanket as well. I desperately want to crawl back into bed with her. I imagine waking her up by slowly sliding inside her, kissing her ear, telling her that I —

You're going to miss your flight, I think.

I lean over her and give her a kiss on the forehead. I imagine that kiss lingering there like a love letter, like a long goodbye, waiting for her when she wakes up.

As I walk down the stairs, I do a mental inventory of all the paperwork I'm leaving in the office. Is it possible that I missed something? Did I double-check my work enough? Maybe I ought to go back in the office and just look at –

Stop it, I berate myself again. *If she wanted you to stay, if she felt the same way about you that you feel about her, she would have* said *something. That's what women do; they voice their feelings. Besides, what could a woman like that want with you, anyway?*

Finally, I reach the bottom of the stairs and then my suitcases are in my hands and I'm in the car.

The engine doesn't start at first, as if even my rental car is saying, *Are you sure?*

That pain in my chest returns and this time there's no pretending that it's heartburn. But I'm sure. At least I'm pretty sure I'm sure. It's too late, now, anyway.

The car's engine turns over. I pull out of the driveway of Mama's house and start driving for the airport. I briefly consider swinging by the Muffin Top. It's barely six AM, but I know Bridgid gets there early to start the baking.

Maybe Regina's said something to Bridgid about me? Maybe Bridgid can tell me what Regina's feelings are, or

I can tell Bridgid what *my* feelings are and then she can tell me if I'm making a terrible mistake in going back to Chicago?

What are you, sixteen? I think and abandon the idea of making the stop.

Instead, I turn the car toward the highway and try to settle in for the journey ahead. I occupy my brain by going over all the steps until I arrive back at my apartment, all alone.

There's this drive back to the airport… then drop off the rental… get the shuttle to the terminal… check in… go through security… grab some fast-food breakfast somewhere and maybe a magazine while I wait to board… the flight back to Chicago… then hop on the El and ride it back to my apartment…

I estimate all of that gives me plenty of time to forget about Regina and that I'll be ready to move on by the time I have to transfer trains in the Loop.

Chapter Thirty-Nine

REGINA

As soon as I wake up I know he's gone.

It's not just that his side of the bed has gone cold beside me. There's also an emptiness in the house that I can feel weighing on me heavier than the blankets. It's oppressive, smothering. Accompanying it is a mocking sort of quiet.

A quiet that I quickly fill with the sounds of my crying. I'm still lying on my side, but the tears flow regardless and soon my pillow is soaked. I cry because he's gone. I cry because I'm never going to see him again. Because I didn't try to stop him. I cry because I'm a coward and I never told him how I felt about him.

Maybe it's not too late, though? Through my watery eyes, I see my cell phone lying on the bedside table. I could call him. Maybe his flight hasn't left. I could woman-up and tell him that I want him to stay. Tell him that I…

But what I wanted was for him to choose *me* over Chicago. If he loved me, that's what he would have done. By leaving, he made his feelings for me abundantly clear. His absence is evidence that he doesn't love me. And ain't that just a double whammy of heartache?

That realization brings with it a whole new wave of tears. I can't believe how badly my heart hurts. I lie on my side and scrunch into a little ball and cry and feel bad for myself and ache over the absence of him.

"Regina?" It's Bridgid's voice, calling from downstairs.

Oh, crap, I think. *What time is it? I should be at the bakery.*

I throw my legs over the side of bed and sit up, hurriedly wiping my tears away. I grab my robe and wrap it around my naked body, cinching it shut.

"Uh-huh, uh-huh," I call back downstairs, "sorry! I'm okay, I was just getting ready to head over…"

My throat constricts and I convulse in another round of tears. I put my hand over my mouth to silence the sounds, not wanting to worry Bridgid.

"Oh, sister…" Bridgid says, suddenly very nearby.

I hear her step into the bedroom. I brush the back of my hands across my face, trying to dry off my cheeks. I sniffle hard and loud. "What are… you doing here?" I ask, trying to keep my voice from shaking and doing a piss poor job of it.

"I locked up for the day already," Bridgid says.

"What? Why?"

"Because. When you didn't show up, I knew what had happened."

I finally look at her. Her face is filled with warmth and sisterly love. So much so that I can't help but start to cry again, falling forward into her embrace.

"He's gone," I wail.

"I know, baby, I know," she comforts me, patting my back.

The questions and self-recriminations fall out of me. "Why'd I let him go? Why didn't he want me? Why did he leave?"

All she can offer are platitudes, but she offers them nonetheless. "It's gonna be okay. He wanted you plenty. I don't know why he left. You'll be alright."

"How?" I ask.

"Here's how."

She picks up a plastic bag and dumps its contents out on the bed. Out comes an assortment of treats from the bakery, as well as all kinds of candy and ice cream. "Let's eat ourselves sick," she snickers, leaning in close and giving me one of her big smiles.

"Why not?" I say, half-laughing and half-choking on my tears.

I grab one of her cream puffs and take a huge bite out of it, getting some of the gooey insides on my nose and chin and enjoying the freedom of not caring.

Then a voice calls from below, shouting, "Hello? Hello?"

"Up here!" Bridgid shouts as I shove another cream puff in my mouth.

A moment later, Trulia is standing in the bedroom doorway. "I heard there was a party going on!"

"Get in here," I say, waving my hand to gesture her to the bed.

"Look out below!" She kicks off her shoes and charges the bed, leaping into the air and doing a full bellyflop onto the bed. Candy and snacks go bouncing into the air and flying every which way as Bridgid and I squeal.

"Gimme some of that," Trulia demands, reaching into the giant pile of goodies. She grabs a candy bar and rips it open with her teeth, growling. I burst into snotty laughter as she snarls and takes a huge bite of candy. "Mmm! Any excuse for a sugar binge and I am in. Only man you need is named Willy Wonka. Or my fearsome twosome, Ben… and his tasty brother Jerry…"

She holds up a tub of ice cream and presses its freezing sides to my bare thigh. I scream in delight and laugh as Trulia goes back to devouring the candy bar.

As my laughter subsides, Bridgid takes my face in her hands. "You're gonna be OK, big sister. I promise you."

"With sisters like these, I think I will be," I tell her.

"We need a Hugh Grant movie or something," Trulia says with her mouth full. "Did Mama get a Netflix subscription or anything?"

"No."

"Hang on! I still got DVDs in my old bedroom!"

Katrina leaps out of bed and goes running for her room, sliding along the floor in her socks. A moment later, she returns and pops a dumb romantic comedy in the DVD player and the three of us are curled up in one big bundle on the bed, sharing snacks and love and sisterhood.

I'm not alone if I've got them, I tell myself.

I haven't forgotten about Michael. And the pain in my heart is still there. But this is better than crying alone in bed, that's for sure.

I try to focus on my sisters, and the sugar, and the movie, and not on him on a plane getting farther and farther away from me…

Chapter Forty

MICHAEL

As the young lady behind the rental desk charges my credit card, I lay the car key on the counter. She's asking me some questions about how my trip was, things like that, to fill the space while the computer processes the transaction. I answer her in single syllables, not really paying attention.

A question of my own keeps nagging at my brain: *What are you doing?*

"What do you mean, what am I doing," I respond silently to myself. "I'm going home."

What's back in Chicago that's worth leaving the love of your life?

"Well," I start to counter inwardly again, "There's my job and my apartment and my... I'm sorry, what did you just say?"

You mean what did you *just say*, my own brain says back to me.

'Love of your life.' Those are the words my brain just used. I kind of dare it to say those words again. It doesn't.

That doesn't matter, though, because my *heart* knows what my brain just said. It commences to beating rapidly against my ribs, as if it were thumping out its own frustrated cry of, "What do you think I've been trying to tell you for the last few days?"

I love her. I love Regina. And when you love somebody, you know what you *don't* do? You don't hop on a fucking plane and fly hundreds of miles away from them!

The rental agent is handing me back my credit card. I see her hand start to reach for the car key. I quickly slap my hand on top of the key, blocking her.

"I'm sorry," I say. "Can I actually *extend* the rental?"

"Well, uh, sure," she says, taken aback. She turns her attention to her computer. "Um, for how long?"

I've already got my suitcases in my hand and I'm halfway out the door as I shout back to her, "Not sure! Maybe indefinitely!"

I laugh as I run through the parking lot, the suitcases swinging in my arms. I toss them into the trunk of the rental, fling myself in the driver's seat and book it back to the house.

The drive takes me past Billy's BBQ. Past the Muffin Top bakery, which I note is curiously closed. I pass through this town that I realize has become – and is meant to be – my home. Eventually, I pull up to the house of – yes! – the woman I love.

I rush up to the front door and realize I've been so focused on getting back, so focused on the pure giddiness of admitting my love for Regina to myself, that I have no idea what I'm going to say to her.

I pause for a moment to try and come up with some words. Something romantic but not sappy, something that tells her how I feel but isn't, y'know, *needy* or anything…

Then I realize there's loud music blaring from inside the house. I hear muffled female voices giving shouts and whoops of joy. The walls of the house are shaking slightly.

She's celebrating my being gone, I think suddenly.

Oh, shut up, I think even more suddenly in return.

Whatever. The words will come when I need them, I suppose. I knock, clear my throat, shake out the excitement in my body and wait for Regina to open the door.

And wait.

And wait some more.

Not exactly how I pictured it. I figured she'd open the door, be shocked but overjoyed to see me, I'd sweep her up in my arms and… I don't know… fade to black or whatever.

I realize she probably can't hear me over the music that's blaring in the hosue. I try the door and find that it's unlocked.

"Uh, hello?"

I make my way inside and push into the living room where I find an impromptu dance party happening. Regina and her sisters are in their socks and PJs, bouncing around the room, limbs going every which way, hair swishing, all of them whooping it up as they jump.

Bridgid is the first one to see me. She stops dancing and grabs Katrina's arm, patting it excitedly. Katrina looks, then hurriedly turns off the music. Regina freezes mid-dance move and starts to ask what's wrong. She comes up short when she sees her sisters' faces.

She turns to discover me.

Her eyes are red-rimmed from crying. Her bottom lip trembles as she sees me. She sinks onto the arm of the nearest chair.

I walk into the living and I don't stop until I'm kneeling in front of her. I grab her smooth, soft hands in mine. "I love you," I say, the words falling out of my mouth in a torrent, like they've been eager to get themselves out into the world. I guess they have. "I love you," I say again, "and I love this house and I love this town and did I mention yet that I love you?"

"Third time," Katrina says, snickering. Bridgid smacks her arm.

"I love you, too," Regina says, her eyes welling with tears.

I feel them come to the surface of my own eyes. "Tell me I can stay."

The tears trickle down her face, leaving little wet trails along her beautiful brown skin. But she laughs, happy, giddy, making me laugh too, as she says, "Yes, yes, you'll always have a home here. Or wherever I am."

"I'm sorry it took so long for me to say it."

"Me, too."

I rise off my knees and pull her into a kiss. Our faces are wet as we touch, but it doesn't matter. The love exploding between us is like fireworks going off. I kiss her and kiss her again, then look in her eyes and kiss her once more, feeling like there aren't enough kisses in the world to express my love for her.

It's a theory I'm willing to put to the test.

We hold each other close, kissing all the while as we blindly make our way upstairs. We never even hear her sisters leave as we move into the bedroom and descend onto the bed, secure in one another's embrace.

I can't wait to spend the rest of my life with this girl.

———

I hope you enjoyed Regina and Michael's story! Looking for more BWWM Interracial Romance? Check out book 3 in the Muffin Top Bakery series, **Triple Down**…

http://bklink.to/tripledown-buy

Trulia Grant left the big city to find herself. Instead, she found a man who helped her discover a whole new world…

Trulia was always the runt of the litter. Out of the three Grant sisters, she was always the quirky one—*different*—and paved her own path no matter the obstacles in her way.

So, it wasn't surprising that she never expected to move back to her close-minded hometown, but that's not all she never expected.

She never expected someone like Tyson Hayes to enter her life.

This white boy is gorgeous, laid back, and has a quiet charm that pulls at her heart. Where Trulia thrived on the energy of New York City, Tyson has a laid back and easy going attitude.

He's not her type, and she's *definitely* not his.

But something brings them together and forces them to crave one another when they're apart.

Can these two figure out what is between them—if these feelings are real–before they get hurt? And hopefully before other people hurt *them?*

http://bklink.to/tripledown-buy

Keep reading for an excerpt...

Trulia

I wake up feeling refreshed and happy, perhaps for the first time since my mother died. Things with her death are finally wrapped up. The bakery is doing good, her estate is settled—things finally feel like they're going back to normal. Now I can actually just focus on the grief without all the extra stuff.

Mama and I weren't as close as my sister Bridgid was with her, but Mama *always* accepted me for who I was. She never judged me, always kept an open mind. Like when I decided that I no longer wanted to be called "Katrina" anymore and told her that I demanded to be called "Trulia." Mama didn't even argue. She just gave me a hug and nodded.

It's lonely not having that person to go to anymore. I've always been independent in my actions, and no one could ever tell me what to do or who to be. But when it came down to it, when I needed help or just someone to talk to about the serious shit in life—I called Mama. And now I can't.

I've been dealing with that ugly truth pretty well if you ask me—but it has definitely affected my art. You see, I'm a visual artist. I moved to New York City shortly after I turned twenty. In New York, I was always able to find some type of job where I could do what I loved. NYC has such a broad spectrum that I never had any trouble with that. But here, in small town Texas—it's much different. *Much* different. And the inspiration has been incredibly lacking lately.

That's why today I've decided to take a little trip to a nearby park that I've been eyeing. I do lots of different types of art—but my favorite thing to do is paint. More specifically, I like to paint nature. Sunsets, moonscapes, beautiful views, flowers etc. It's what I feel the most at peace doing. So when I'm looking for a little more inspiration for a piece, I like to walk around in nature and take pictures of things that I find beautiful. Then I can look through them when I get home and see if I like any of them enough to paint.

On my way to the park, I turn on my favorite R&B station to get myself into a more creative mood. Once there, I pull out my favorite and only professional camera and begin my walk. Luckily, it's a beautiful day, so it doesn't take long before inspiration strikes. I'm able to snap a couple good shots before my phone rings.

Ugh, it's James—my sort-of boyfriend back in New York. I say sort of because we aren't technically official—meaning we're both allowed to see other people (which I know he does).

The arrangement seemed fine at first—no strings or feelings involved. But James seems to like the no-commitment thing a bit too much for my taste. I kind of thought that by now we would've turned into something more. So lately when he calls, it takes everything in me not to just decline the connection.

"Hey babe, what's up?" I reluctantly answer.

"Hey Tru, it's been a minute since I heard your voice. It almost seems like you're busier now than you were in The Big Apple."

My mother just died, you dipshit—of course I've been busy.

"Yeah, it's been a little crazy. But things are settling down now."

"Oh yeah? How's the small-town life treatin' you?"

"Oh you know, it's pretty boring. Not really my style, as you know."

"Yeah, I'll bet. When you comin' back to the city? It misses you."

"I'm actually not sure right now. Something seems to be pulling me to stay here a bit longer."

Awkward silence.

"So how have you been?" I ask.

"Good, good…"

"That's good."

Things seem to get more and more boring with each conversation we have. It's like without me there, we've just run out of things to say, or forgotten how to speak altogether.

"How are your sisters?"

"Good, they're good."

"No more screaming matches?"

"Oh no, things have calmed down a whole lot. They're both actually really happy right now."

"Sounds pretty boring. At least when they were screaming it was fun to watch."

"Yeah… I guess."

Awkward silence.

"You know, James—I'm actually in the middle of trying to find some art inspo right now. Could I call you back later?"

"Yeah, for sure. I got some stuff to do anyway. Talk later, bye."

"Bye."

I hang up, with no intent to call him back any time soon.

It's not that James isn't generally a nice, handsome man. He is, it's just that we aren't really on the same page in any aspect of our lives. He seems to be perfectly content with the "relationship" we have, and I most certainly am not. I'd rather be single than have something this meaningless.

So why haven't I ended it? Well, I keep telling myself that I shouldn't make decisions like this while I'm in the midst of my grief. Especially because I'm kind of known to be quite an impulsive person. I'm trying to improve on that part of myself. But truthfully, I know that I should end it. I'm not really sure what's keeping me from doing it.

After our phone call, I just feel even more lonely than I did beforehand. As I'm encroaching on thirty-four, I find myself craving a real partner. Something more. Especially after seeing both of my sisters fall in love in less than a year.

I'm honestly a little jealous of them, and maybe even a little sad. For the first time probably ever, all three of us are getting along perfectly. And at the same time, both Bridgid and Regina have found the men of their dreams, leaving me even more alone. It's just my luck, too. There's nothing worse than watching everyone around you being perfectly happy when you're the most miserable you've ever been.

Stuffing my camera back in my bag, I give up and head back to my car. I'm certainly in no mood to be doing this now, I'll have to try again tomorrow.

http://bklink.to/tripledown-buy

About the Author

Hey readers! I'm Tasha Hart, author of contemporary romances. Thanks for reading my stories. From a young age, I've been inspired to tell stories about the ideas I have all the time. It started with telling wild stories, then some wilding of my own... but now I'm settling down with some good coffee and trying to write great books. It's a lot like running, which is what I usually do to figure out how my characters are going to misbehave. Totally distracting, consumes me wholly in the moment, and then it feels like magic! If you like reading my stories, consider pushing the Amazon follow button so you'll get notified when I've got a new book release!

Find Tasha online at… https://tashahart.com